BISON
BOOKS

Other Novels by Mildred Walker
Available in Bison Books Editions

THE CURLEW'S CRY

FIREWEED

IF A LION COULD TALK

LIGHT FROM ARCTURUS

THE QUARRY

THE SOUTHWEST CORNER

UNLESS THE WIND TURNS

WINTER WHEAT

Dr. Norton's Wife

BY MILDRED WALKER

Introduction to the Bison Books Edition
by David Budbill

University of Nebraska Press
Lincoln and London

Manufactured in the United States of America

⊗ The paper in this book meets the minimum requirements
of American National Standard for Information Sciences—
Permanence of Paper for Printed Library Materials,
ANSI Z39.48-1984.

First Bison Books printing: 1996
Most recent printing indicated by the last digit below:
10 9 8 7 6 5 4 3 2 1

Library of Congress Cataloging-in-Publication Data
Walker, Mildred, 1905–
Dr. Norton's wife / by Mildred Walker; introduction to the
Bison Books edition by David Budbill.
p. cm.
ISBN 0-8032-9782-3 (pa: alk. paper)
I. Title.
PS3545.A524D7 1996
813′.52—dc20
95-53292 CIP

for my husband

INTRODUCTION

David Budbill

In a recent article in the *Boston Sunday Globe* (16 July 1995) about the purpose and current state of art in America, Ed Siegel says there is a depressingly large and "growing number of artists who think it is enough simply to reflect the violence of the day." Then Siegel quotes National Public Radio commentator James Isaacs, "An element of being [an artist] used to be culling beauty from sadness. Now the attitude is 'let's just reflect the overall ugliness around us.'" Within this dark, violent, and sarcastic take on things, humanity has become a wretched and hopeless collection of conniving miscreants and opportunistic sleazeballs who are helpless to do anything but torture each other to the grave.

This sophisticated, fashionably gloomy, and above all misanthropic view of humanity is what I like to call "chic bleak." Why this view of ourselves has so much credence just now is an interesting question and one that cannot be pursued here. Suffice it to say that in other times—and times *at least* as dark as ours—other artists have drawn other conclusions about the nature of humanity. In 1947 Albert Camus at the end of *The Plague*, a novel about Nazism, says, "We learn in a time of pestilence that there is more to admire in men than to despise." And quite a few years before Camus, Sophocles says, in *Antigone*, "Numberless are the world's wonders, and none more wonderful than man." And before Sophocles the ancient Chinese poets sang praises to our species also and in times of their own as dark as any we have ever known. It is curious how differently various artists and ages can perceive the purpose, function, and effect of suffering and darkness. Now, again, into this struggle to understand human nature and destiny steps the quiet and mild-mannered, soft-spoken and plain Mildred Walker with this reprint of her third novel, originally published in 1938, *Dr. Norton's Wife.*

As the story begins, Sue Norton, an invalid and Dr. Dan Norton's wife, is in bed with an unspecified degenerative and debilitating disease. Not until the reader is forty-five pages into the story does Mildred Walker reveal for the first time, and the last, that Sue Norton has multiple sclerosis. The arduous and painful accuracy with which Walker describes the symptoms of the disease, the disease's advance, and its brutal effect on Sue Norton's body and mind are so precisely done that when *Dr. Norton's Wife* was first published it was used as a teaching tool in medical schools. But there is nothing clinical about this story. This is a story of love and death.

Because of the demands of Sue Norton's disease and in order to help out, Sue's sister, the recently divorced Jean Keller, comes to live with Sue and Dan. Jean is healthy and beautiful, full of vivacity and wit, and, in fact, looks a lot like Sue did before the disease changed Sue's mind into a pale imitation of what it used to be, her body into a stumbling, jerking, unmanageable enemy, and her face into an expressionless mask.

Then the inevitable: Jean falls in love with Dan. Given a lesser writer, such a plot would become little more than soap opera, but in Mildred Walker's serious and loving hands this triangle, the agony of Sue's debilitating disease and the resulting struggle to do what is good and right, becomes a story of loneliness and anguish before the incurable. It becomes what Edith Wharton and her mentor Henry James believed was the only serious purpose for any novel: a discussion of the importance and complexity of moral values and ethical choices in our lives.

This is a novel of contrasts. Mildred Walker paints scenes so that the brutal reality of Sue Norton's life as an invalid will stand out in the starkest possible way. On the novel's broadest canvas Walker paints a picture of Dan Norton, the young, lively, brilliant, and successful doctor in a teaching hospital in a university town, burdened with a sick wife. Around these two swirl the ambitious younger doctors and their wives. Walker minces no words when describing the nature of this isolated, self-congratulatory, academic community where the self-satisfied and smug brim over with confidence that nothing so untoward as what has happened to Sue Norton could possibly happen to them. Yet Sue Norton hovers there at the edges of those other beautiful lives as crippled, living proof that tragedy constantly lurks in the shadows even if the young and the ambitious have neither time nor eyes to see it. Sue Norton's illness, disability, rage, and grief is, to change metaphors, an ever-present and ominous drone sounding in the lives of the youthful, ambitious, and successful people all around her.

At one point early in the story, Peter Whitney, the best and brightest of the young doctors working under the tutelage of Dan Norton, says of Sue's illness, "It's a horrible thing! You can see what a strain Dan's under. Think of a blow like that falling on him when he's right at the top of his profession!" Little does Peter Whitney know when he makes his self-possessed declaration what fate has waiting for him less than a year away. There is more than a little here about the doctor's wife as an accouterment to the doctor's career. Even the title of this book can be seen as a statement regarding Sue Norton's place in the scheme of things in this medical-academic world.

And in miniature Mildred Walker also illustrates this same stark contrast between the sick and the well. One evening Dan comes into Sue's room with proofs of an article he has written for a medical journal. They will do as they used to do. Sue will help him correct the proofs and then, also as they used to do, they will eat apples. But Sue cannot control the pencil in her hand. Her hand shakes. Her line scrawls. She can't make her pencil move into the space between the words. Her mind can't follow the logic of the article. And after only a few minutes she is exhausted. In the end "Her corrections were vague lines such as a child might make" (65). Dan goes to fetch the apples:

> He came back up from the basement with a plate of apples. He whistled all the way. He sat by her and pared the apple so carefully the peeling fell in one long red curl. . . . He cut the apple into thin slivers and passed her one on the blade of the knife.
>
> "It's so good, Dan."
>
> "Northern Spy; there's nothing better." But when he took a bite himself, pity spoiled the flavor. (65–66)

Again and again Mildred Walker lets us see these contrasts, Dan's simple and amazing dexterity with a knife, Sue's inability with a pencil. Again and again we see how far Sue Norton's life is from ordinary, normal human activity.

And we see also what a burden her life is on the lives of those around her, and how those around her are confused by their own feelings of condescension and pity toward Sue. Jean, for example, loves and wants to care for her sister, but she finds herself unwittingly doing and saying things that make the situation worse for Sue.

Sue's sharpened awareness of people's new feelings toward her complicates things further. During an evening's attempt at bridge Sue notices how much more observant and critical of other people she has become:

> They were . . . pretending to gaiety, making their voices eager. Had she always used to notice the tone of people's voices so carefully, or just since her own had lost all tone? . . . They were anxious to compliment her, so careful not to seem to see her slow, painful movements. . . . She saw them suddenly as three adults who had been amusing a child for the evening. She had been the only one really engrossed. Perhaps they had even let her win. She wanted to drop the cards, to tell them it was no fun for her either. (147–50)

And to the falsely nonchalant and inadvertently condescending comments the others make to entertain and amuse Sue, Walker tells us:

> The trite words sounded hollow in Sue's ears. There was something almost indecent about these casual remarks used to cover over their boredom.
>
> "I'll go down and make you a hot toddy, Sue, and then tuck you in," Jean said in the tone of the capable, well person to an invalid. Sue hated it at the same time that she was ashamed of her own feeling. (150–51)

And so it goes by turns, this oscillation between hatred and rage for the way she is treated, then shame at her feelings.

When Sue realizes that Dan and Jean are in love—long before anyone else suspects she knows—Sue's frustration and rage explode one moment only to be replaced the next by understanding for this impossible situation in which they are all trapped. Meanwhile in and through all these feelings of rage and sympathy, understanding and jealousy courses the ever-present helplessness Sue feels.

Eventually one evening when Jean and Dan are alone together, Jean confesses openly her love for him, they embrace and kiss; then Dan pulls away. Sue lies, helpless and awake, upstairs knowing somehow all that is going on downstairs. A few days later while they are away from the house Jean confronts Dan:

> "Dan, didn't it mean anything to you, the other night?"
>
> Dan's hand tightened on her arm. She looked up at him quickly and was startled out of herself by the sternness of his expression. He looked older and so tired.
>
> "Dan, I'm sorry, shall we go home and have tea with Sue?" she asked gently. Dan nodded.
>
> "Jean, there isn't anything to do but to go on as we are while Sue lives; we mustn't think of ourselves." (166)

After a couple of decades of the Me Generation such a statement sounds revolutionary. Jean responds:

> "We can't help but think about ourselves, Dan," Jean burst out. "You know we can't. Why can't we recognize that we love each other? . . . I love Sue, too. This sickness of hers is a horrible, ghastly thing, but we can't let it ruin our lives, too." (166)

Thus the issue is joined which tears at and agonizes the three of them. Again and again Walker asks, "[Can] love stand death and separation, but not disease?" (181). One thinks again of Edith Wharton both in her fiction and her life and how she too confronted this same question of what happens when illness and infirmity attack love.

Walker paints both women with a loving and dark realism as they struggle with each other for Dan's love and attention. Jean is devoted to Sue, but she also wants Sue out of the way so she and Dan can have a life together. Sue discovers that in spite of her insurmountable disadvantage she can overcome her helplessness and loneliness and her awareness of Dan's "infidelity" by letting the poison of jealousy make her "giddy with hate" (248).

At the beginning of the novel everyone is full of self-confidence. Even Sue believes she will get well. But slowly everyone, especially Dan Norton, must confront the incurable, unsolvable problem of Sue's disease. The smug self-confidence with which the novel begins—everyone's belief that strength, intelligence, science, and modern medicine can solve any problem—is replaced by the end with a sober acknowledgment that we do not control our circumstances, that we can do little to save ourselves from our fate. Dan comes to understand that, "Circumstances shaped you whether you were weak or strong" (236).

Yet noble Dan Norton struggles on to do what is good and right.

> It wasn't that he had ceased to love Sue, he told himself over and over again. It was that her condition turned his love into pity. . . . Jean was so alive to every mood and feeling. Jean loved him.
>
> Dan lit a cigarette as he drove. To say that there was no difference between infidelity of the mind and body was stupid. Loyalty to Sue, some inherent moral sense had held him back tonight. . . . But, after all, he was no better than the next man, driven by loneliness and hopelessness. That was what sent a man to find comfort in someone else. It was nothing so simple as desire. (238–39)

Wise words these. Yet I keep wondering if Dan Norton isn't too good. How can he remain so loyal and true? How can he resist the temptations of the flesh, the relaxation and kind comfort of another loving, sexual body and soul to hold on to? How can Dan Norton resist so much! If this is Mildred Walker's definition of what true husbandly love for a woman and a wife is, how many of us men can measure up? On the other hand, Walker's understanding of men is far from naive. She knows us perhaps better than many of us know ourselves. She knows us and exposes us, "Personal vanity bulked large in the best of men, disguised under ambition, under sensitiveness, under driving-power" (101).

Stylistically, this novel possesses an odd and beautiful plainness, so plain, in fact, that the sentences themselves help create the stark reality of Sue's illness. In this age of hyperbole and overblown rhetoric, Mildred Walker's quiet modesty can go unnoticed. It is at our peril that we ignore her. Her restrained and delicate way of approaching things is refreshing and satisfying, and something we need to attend to. One day Sue falls into a reverie of days past, days when she and Dan were young and happy, and in the reverie, if only for a moment, she can understand how attractive Jean's healthy mind and body must be to Dan.

> Sue lay still thinking that sometimes just to watch Jean made her feel as though she, herself, were lithe and quick. But when Agnes [her nurse] struggled to get her arms into the dress and her limbs were rigid and jerked unmanageably that feeling left her. It was no wonder that Dan turned away from her to Jean, she told herself bitterly.
>
> But Dan had loved her body. "I could write my own song of Solomon about you, Sue," he had said. He had kissed her shoulders and her breasts and her thighs. "'Tisn't 'beasty,' Sue," he had whispered. And it wasn't; how well she knew now. (204)

The delicate loveliness, the sweet modesty of using "thighs" as a euphemism is irresistibly attractive.

Dr. Norton's Wife is kin to Greek tragedy. What happens externally, in the plot, the action, is significant only as it reveals character by forcing the characters into ethical choices. It is what happens internally, within the hearts and souls of the characters, that makes this novel so valuable and interesting. And in this regard, Mildred Walker is a master of what theatre people call "subtext"—that which is thought and felt but not said. In an odd way, not thematically but stylistically, *Dr. Norton's Wife* reminds me of Eugene O'Neill's *Long Day's Journey into Night.*

This is not a modernist novel in which the artist watching herself make art becomes the subject. Here, instead, is an unabashed selflessness in the face of the importance of the subject. And that selflessness, it seems, reached into all aspects of Mildred Walker's life. In the 1981 edition of *Contemporary Authors,* the entry for Mildred Walker Schemm includes the following statement:

> [The issues I feel are vital include] the necessity for World peace, the protection and reverence for the natural world if we are to survive and the generations after us. I feel strongly about the need to oppose materialism in both our national and individual life—the importance of the freedom of *every* individual, but the need for a better understanding of the nature of freedom—the need to dethrone success as the American ideal and substitute for it a creative quality in our daily living. These are too big and too general to be meaningful set down this way—but how else, except in a novel?

This declaration could be a manifesto for us all.

In the end I believe *Dr. Norton's Wife* is about more than

a particular incurable disease called multiple sclerosis; it is about The Great Incurable Disease: Death, and about the different rates of speed with which, and the various kinds of vehicles on which, we all travel toward our individual ends. Sue Norton debilitates and degenerates before our eyes. Dan Norton does so also, only much more slowly; he ages, grows weary and tired and sober. Like the rest of us, he laments the passing of his youth. He clings to the young doctors and their wives, loves them all passionately, because he wants to be with the youth they have and he has lost. And there are others in this story also who are healthy one minute and dead the next, taken away with sudden and incomprehensible cruelty. Isn't Mildred Walker telling us that we all are caught up in a disease like Sue Norton's, only some of us take more time or less to make it to the end?

If we could understand life and death in this context, as a progressive disease not unlike Sue Norton's malady—an understanding, by the way, the ancient Chinese poets all possessed—perhaps we could better accept those around us with diseases like Sue's, and perhaps also we would be more modest and self-effacing, melancholy and gentle about our own achievements and successes being as they seem so paltry in the face of The Great Incurable Disease to which we all succumb.

And if we were able to adopt this kind of modesty in the face of the inevitable, then the dark and violent, arch and strident "chic bleak" might seem little more than silly. We might be able to see "chic bleak" as a perverted Romanticism which produces its own one-dimensional sentimentality.

Mildred Walker's earnest and kind-hearted, clear-eyed and therefore unsentimental view of the world avoids such extremes and achieves instead a golden mean in which we can see wholly and realistically the incurability of the human condition and the nobility of the human struggle to deal with that condition. Simply put, Mildred Walker culls beauty from sadness.

And in this sad beauty there emerges—I don't know how— a forbearance, a way to embrace love and darkness, grief and kindness, suffering and joy, jealousy and delight, a way to know that we, all of us, are in this boat together headed for the other side.

PART ONE

"I am not only ashamed, but heartily sorry, that, besides death, there are diseases incurable."

"Men that look no farther than their outsides, think health an appurtenance unto life, . . . but I that have examined the parts of man know upon what tender filaments that Fabrick hangs."

SIR THOMAS BROWNE
Religio Medici
CIRCA 1635

SUE NORTON woke early. She could just make out the hands on the mantel clock. It was quarter of five.

She shifted heavily in bed trying to free herself from the mattress that was so different from the mattress on her own bed. This one had been on the hospital bed when they brought it over. The mattress changed queerly during the day. It was deceitfully comfortable after her bath, then during the morning it grew hard until, after a whole night, it pressed up against her mercilessly.

Now it was ten of five, eleven minutes of five, really. She who had never had time for accuracy before was growing painfully accurate. A queer necessity lay upon her to know at exactly what minute Anna went downstairs to start breakfast, Agnes brought her tray, Dan came in, went out; the mailman dropped the mail into the box on the post, the grocery boy came running, running carelessly on sound legs, along the side of the house to the back door. Jean had told the grocery boy once to come in from the rear but she had missed him and sent Agnes down to ask him to come in along the side path so she could hear him running by.

Now it was exactly ten minutes of five. She threw back the sheet and blanket a minute. The October air was cold. It came through the thin silk of her gown, over her flesh like a wave of cold water. She breathed in deeplv, feeling herself bathed in the cold air. Being bathed by Agnes in water that was always tepid wasn't a bath at all.

She reached out and pulled up the sheet and blanket and the warmth was delicious now. She dropped her head against one shoulder and shivered with the satisfaction of warmth. Then she lay still again watching the leaves of the wistaria vine that climbed the eaves spout. The morning light was a bluish white like the glass of Dan's thermometer. Soon the mornings would be dark at five; five minutes of five, it was.

Sue didn't mind waking so early. There was all day to think in now, but the day's thinking was controlled, altered, obstructed by so many things: people, irritations, fatigue and discomfort. Now, early in the morning, her thoughts were free. She felt better in the morning than all day long. She wished Dan would come in at this time in the day, before anyone else was awake. They never seemed to be alone any more. Always when Dan came in, later in the morning, or at noon, or before dinner, the sounds of the life going on in the rest of the house came to them, pulling Dan away from her.

But Dan slept soundest early in the morning. She had used to waken sometimes, not this early, not at five o'clock, but earlier than Dan, and look over at him, sleeping on his side, his face on his hand. If she stirred nearer to him he would put out his arm without waking and she would move closer and fall asleep against him.

What if she should get out of bed? If she took her time and rested, she could manage; she could pull herself along the hall into Dan's room. If she went very slowly she wouldn't stumble. Now, when she was rested, early in the morning, perhaps she could even control the tremor in her hands and her unruly legs. Nobody would hear her. Dan had said she was so much better. Jean and Agnes would be so surprised when they found her out of her room. Jean would exclaim, her voice rising to a little crescendo, "Why, Sue, how wonderful!"

But it was only Dan who mattered. Dan would wake suddenly, in that quick way he did when the phone rang in the night. He would love having her come to him; he would love having her well again. That set, patient look he had sometimes on his face would go. She lay enjoying the thought until it seemed reality.

It was unbelievable that Dan Norton's wife should be an invalid, practically bed-ridden. That happened to other faculty men's wives. There was the wife of the man in the literary school who was hopelessly crippled by arthritis. At the Faculty Women's Club they had moved every year for years to send her flowers. She, herself, when she was secretary, had sometimes gone down and picked them out. And then there was the philosophy man's wife who went insane and, of course, Mrs. Blodgett, whose porch had an inclined plane up one side of the front steps so that she could be easily wheeled out in the garden. But that Dan Norton's wife should be an invalid was fantastic.

She had always been so well, so energetic. There was that sabbatical year they had spent in England. They had bicycled miles through Cornwall and people told them afterwards that Cornwall was too full of hills.

Of course, she had never been able to have a child after that dreadful miscarriage; but many women couldn't have children, and she and Dan had been all the closer.

It was quarter after five. If she were going to try it . . . But she lay still against the pillow. She must get up without thinking so much about it; her muscles worked better when she didn't try so hard. She must just slip of of bed the way anyone would, the way she used to do before that awful day last year.

It was at the annual tea for the wives of the new doctors. She had been pouring at the other end of the table from Stella Ridley; Tad Cooper's wife was standing by her, when the cream pitcher slipped out of her fingers, clattering against the silver tray, splashing over on her dress, even spotting Mrs. Cooper's dress. People looked up quickly and then went right on talking. The maid took the pitcher out and Mrs. Cooper laughed and said, "I was talking too much, Mrs. Norton." She had tried to go on pouring, thinking it was only because she was upset that her hand was so unsteady. Finally she had begged off, whispering to Alice Hutchins that she had a headache, which was a lie. She had always been proud that she didn't get headaches.

Afterwards, driving over to the hospital for Dan, she had felt all right.

"Did you get the new wives baptized in tea?" Dan had asked.

"Almost literally, Dan." She had laughed and told him about the pitcher. And Dan had been amused and said that must have helped to break the ice. When they reached home they left the car in the driveway and went up the steps together and then, inconceivably, she had stumbled over the sill.

"I'm getting clumsy," she had said. The words were cut into her memory. Dan had given her a swift, keen look that made her feel uneasy.

At dinner she had felt him watching her. "How have you been feeling lately, Sue?"

"Why, fine; oh, a little tired, maybe; I always get tired when you stay for summer school."

That had been the beginning of everything. Stephen Ridley came home with Dan, as if by chance, and asked her questions as though she were a patient. He had held a pencil up and made her follow it with her eyes until she had laughed and objected. In the winter her right foot began to drag when she walked.

Why must she go back like this over the whole slow, yet terribly fast series of events that had led to this present helplessness? Tag ends of sentences stayed in her mind, jumping out at her suddenly as they had the day they were spoken, like telegrams she had saved along with old letters: Dan looking at her that day he took her out for a drive, trying to be casual about it, yet with his purpose showing through his words, "let's drive out the river road a ways, Sue." She had known that day how he must look to patients; his eyes steady and his lips coming together gravely.

"It's going to be a long pull, Sue. It might develop into something very serious unless you're careful and keep rested and don't worry." His voice had been so kindly . . . to her! It was the kindliness in his voice that had frightened her so. She had started to cry and Dan had stopped the car to comfort her.

"But, Dan, I don't see what caused it. Will I be sick long?" She could still remember her own words and Dan saying,

"We aren't sure of the cause, darling." And Dan was telling the truth; he didn't lie. "There are some theories that it's caused by a focus of infection some place in the body, but the boys who believe that are upset by the fact that when you remove every possible focus there are still cases that . . . when it's all boiled down, Sue, we just don't know." He had been so bothered that, in spite of all the things she wanted to ask, she was quiet. Dan let the car into gear but he drove with one hand hard on hers.

"But I'm going to get well, Dan?" she had asked finally.

"Of course, Sue, only you'll have to be patient, and

there may be some slight stiffness. I don't believe you'll ever dance quite so beautifully, but then, when you think of the things that happen to people, Sue, that's very little."

It was lucky that Jean had been on for a visit and could stay and run the house until she was well again. Then Dan had brought home a nurse, but she had grown so used to her, Agnes Barton hardly seemed like a nurse. It was really only last March that she, herself, had been moved into this sewing-room where the radio was and the Sunday *Times* used to lie around for a week, and the set of encyclopedias and the dictionary used to be stored. It seemed longer than that since she had moved from their room in the front of the house to this room that was just across from the bathroom and the little room Agnes used and had become a "conveniently arranged invalid."

Now it was five-thirty. Still there was no sound in the house. It was hard to tell whether the day would be clear or cloudy in the morning mist. It really mattered very little, one way or another. Nothing mattered except to break the cage that this sickness had thrown up around her. Since her illness even she and Dan were changing. It was hard to be quite natural any more; hard to feel close to Dan.

It was quarter of six.

She leaned forward until she could see herself in the mirror over the dresser. She could see only a shadowy image: a pale face, the dark hair falling loosely over her shoulders. She pushed her hair back with her hands and tried to arrange it around her face. Her hand trembled so she brought it down to lie on the bed to rest it. She reached stiffly for the dressing gown that lay on the foot of the bed and pulled it around her, trying to busy her mind with that, to trick her mind so she could slip out of the high bed without thinking about it.

It was cold out of bed. The heat wouldn't come up in the radiator for another hour but the half light and silence in the room seemed to intrigue with her. She found her slipper with her foot and got it on. That was pretty good. Of course, she could do it. The right one was harder. It went on crookedly. She had to lean against the bed. It took endless time to straighten it with fingers that shook as they reached her foot. There!

She had not really seen Dan for so long. Sometimes when she heard him come in the front door after she had been waiting just for that his coming was spoiled by Jean's calling out,

"Hello, Dan, run on up and see Sue."

Jean didn't need to tell him. He would anyway. Jean said it without thinking how it sounded; her clear voice carried upstairs so easily.

It was ten after six Sue noticed as she reached the hall door. She wished she had started sooner instead of lying there thinking. She wanted fiercely to lie beside

Dan and talk with him the way they always used to do in the morning before they got up.

When she had moved into the hospital bed in the sewing-room (it would always go on being the sewing-room to her) Dan had said,

"You'll be more comfortable, Sue; your regime can go on better and it will only be for a little while."

She hadn't objected. She had felt so sick then. But now she was getting well. And she missed Dan so terribly. Dan was there, but when he came to see her he made a call, a kind of visit; even when he stretched out on the couch and smoked his pipe. And he was gone before she wanted him to go, always. She had to speak so slowly these days and Dan grew impatient. She could see it in the way his eyes glanced around and the way he held himself to listen.

This morning she wouldn't try to talk. Dan would just hold her close. She remembered the time, before she had moved into the sewing-room, when Dan had reached over to her and held her the way he used to before she was sick, held her so tightly her body ached. He had kissed her eyes and her mouth and her shoulder and then he had remembered suddenly and been afraid that he had hurt her.

Her foot dragged, making a scraping sound over the carpet. Slowly she helped herself past the book-case in the hall. Now she could see the glass knob of Dan's door. It sparkled in the dark hall. Jean was in their old room. Dan had moved into the east room.

"I don't want to be there without you, dear," Dan had said.

The hallway turned to make a wider space around the well of the stairs. The length of the hall was a long way. She was tired already. If she could sit down, just for a minute, but then her stiff legs would never get her up and she would have to sit there until Agnes found her. She must keep on. Dan was there; just a little way now. Dan's face would light up so; she would open the door and just whisper his name. She whispered it now to give her strength. "Dan!"

She came to the hall table with its night lamp on it, just as it always used to be. She reached out to steady herself by it, but she was too heavy for the table. It tipped with her. The lamp crashed on the floor and she fell sprawling on top of the pieces, still clutching at one side of the table. She let go of the table but she was too tired to try to lift herself up. It was no use now. She had waked the whole house. She turned her face against the floor with a moan.

"Sue! Darling, are you hurt?" Dan was lifting her in his arms.

"I didn't hear her, and my door was ajar," Agnes said. "I'm so sorry, Mrs. Norton. Was there something you wanted?" Agnes looked so worried.

Sue shook her head hopelessly.

"Sue, dear!" Jean came running out from her bedroom, tying her scarlet negligee as she came. Sue watched her quick steps over Dan's shoulder.

"Darling, what did you want?" Dan was whispering to her.

"Oh, Dan, I . . ." She was so tired she could scarcely make her words. They came more slowly than usual, with that hateful staggering. She couldn't help it; better not try to talk. The foolish tears that had come to her eyes were drying now. Dan looked so sleepy still.

Dan laid her down on the hospital bed. Agnes was covering her.

"Darling, you mustn't try that again alone." But Dan spoke very gently. Agnes had gone to close the window. Now she was stooping to light the gas fire. Jean had been fixing the table in the hall. She came into the room. Sue lay still waiting for them to go, wanting to be alone with Dan.

How helpless she must have looked, lying there on the hall floor! Dan's finger was on her pulse. She was a patient.

"Dan . . ." Her voice came out in a quaver.

"I'll be here with Mrs. Norton," Dan said to Agnes.

"Oh, Dan, let me, you were so tired last night," Jean murmured in a low voice.

Sue closed her eyes and turned away. "I'll sleep

now," she managed to say. She could feel them lingering. They could all go, even Dan.

But Dan sat by her bed after Jean had gone. Now she could tell him how lonely she was. She could keep him here and pretend that their life was as it always had been, pretend that she had never been sick. She opened her eyes.

Dan did look tired. He stooped and kissed her gently; not like that time when he had been afraid he had hurt her.

"You mustn't try too much at first, Sue. Take it easy a little while longer." He smiled. She couldn't smile back. She closed her eyes because she could feel the tears gathering again, but Dan took it for weariness. He pulled up the covers around her shoulders, gently, ever so gently. He laid his hand on her forehead and smoothed back her hair. But she felt that he was only waiting for her to sleep before he went back to his own day.

It was all spoiled now. The soft, secret feeling of the early morning was gone. She couldn't get to Dan; only as far as the little table that stood in the hall.

Now it was quarter of seven.

2

DAN went back to his room and lay down again on the bed, trying to rid himself of the picture of Sue stumbling around the house in the early morning; of the helpless, almost baffled look on her face.

He had always been relieved that there had been no signs of mental impairment in Sue. But this morning he wondered whether it would not be more merciful if her mind were dulled so that she could not realize how pitifully weak her body had become.

Only yesterday he had talked with Stephen Ridley about her. Stephen's clinical judgment was equal to that of any man in the country. Stephen's words came back to him:

"You know as well as I do that the fever therapy hasn't done anything for her. There's no use fooling ourselves, Dan. What little improvement she showed I believe was a natural remission of the disease."

He had known all that, but he had hidden the truth from himself until Stephen confirmed it.

"I think the hypodermic injections should go on; we mustn't have Sue feel that there's nothing being done. We want her to feel that she's improving, unless, of course, you think . . ."

"Oh, no, Stephen!" he had said quickly. He couldn't have Sue knowing that she would get no better; that she would seem better for an interval and then slowly grow worse again until another remission. The disease advanced as its victims walked, with a staggering gait. Sue was made for life and health; she could never stand knowing that she couldn't get well. He could never tell her. She took things so hard.

There was that time after she had lost the baby. . . . He closed his eyes tightly against the picture that forced its way upon him so vividly he seemed to be seeing Sue again. He had talked to Roberts that day just as he had talked to Stephen yesterday, only it had been in the spring instead of fall; their second spring in Woodstock.

He had meant to tell Sue what Roberts said, but he put it off all through dinner. After dinner he settled himself on the old davenport that they used to drag up to the open window of the apartment and say it was as good as having a porch. He tried to do some studying. He did a lot of studying that first year. Sue brought a book and curled up at the other end of the davenport, leaning against his knees.

"Dan! Oh, I'm sorry, never mind."

"What?" She was always so contrite about interruptions.

"Nothing, only I just remembered I gained a pound this week. That ought to please Dr. Roberts." He had told her she must build up her general strength.

"Good for you, Sue."

Then suddenly her body that had lain lazily against his knees was tense. She turned around and faced him.

"Dan, did Dr. Roberts say something? I mean, did

he say . . ." He would never know how she sensed what was in his mind, almost as though she sensed it through his body.

"He said, dear . . ." He told her exactly. It never occurred to him then to keep anything from her. He and Sue were too close. "Roberts said he didn't think it *probable* that you would have any children, darling . . . but he doesn't know everything, Sue."

"Enough to be head of Obstetrics," she answered in a small, wintry voice.

She flung away from him across the room so he couldn't see her face. He watched her, not knowing whether she wanted to be alone or not. He had expected her to burst into tears, but when she spoke her voice was quiet, almost impersonal.

"Barren, Dan, is such an ugly word. It makes you feel . . . half there. Oh, Dan, you'll always feel cheated."

"Sue, look at me!"

She had come then with a rush and hid her face against him like a child until he lifted it up to kiss her. Her whole slim body was shaking; it was no child's weeping.

"Sue, know this; I'll never feel cheated as long as I have you."

"You can't be sure, Dan," she had whispered. "Anyhow I feel cheated." She talked to him with her face hidden against him. He had snapped off the light and pulled her up into his arms. They had sat there until long after the whole apartment was still and even the fraternity house back of them had quieted down. He thought of that evening sometimes when he drove past the old Abernathy Apartments and looked up to the narrow balcony on the third floor.

Once she had sat up straight and beat against his shoulder with hard fists. "Dan, it's so unjust, though." It was unjust. Why should Sue of all women . . . and then he had thought of an answer.

"But, Sue, some women have children and never know what love like ours is."

"Dan, I know it," she had whispered and lain back against him.

Some boys coming home late along Fourth Street sang out in a sudden raucous burst, "I need sy-ym-pathy . . ." dragging out the words in exaggeration of some vaudeville singer. He had almost held his breath; it was too pat. Sue was in no mood for the ridiculous. But then she had sat up and giggled, and he knew that she had taken that hurdle. "I need sympathy" had been a pass word between them ever since.

Why had he gone all over that again? But that was the way his mind shuttled back and forth between Sue as she used to be and now. There was no good in that. He turned his head slowly from side to side. His head ached as though he had been up all night or had slept in a close room.

Ridley had suggested yesterday that he take half a semester and go away somewhere with Sue. But that would make her think of other sabbatical years. It was true that the thought of another year, breaking in new instructors in his department, creating a new morale, only added to his weariness. But there was no use going away. Sue wouldn't be so comfortable as at home, and it would do no good. If he had gone into private practice instead of being professor of medicine they might go away to some medical center for confirmation of diagnosis, but, as it was, it was foolish to go some place else.

They would just go on quietly another fall and another winter. Any change in Sue's condition would come slowly, creeping up on them as Time did here in Woodstock. Already it was twenty years ago this fall since he had married Sue and come here as Junior instructor.

He heard Jean up in the next room. Dishes rattled on the stairs. Agnes was taking Sue's breakfast to her. He would go in and see how she felt; then he remembered; Sue didn't want him there when she had her meals. It was too difficult for her to eat without spilling. His mind shrank from the thought of Sue having to suffer that indignity. He shuffled across the hall to the bathroom. A shower might take away the dog-tired feeling that clung to him so much of the time.

When he came downstairs Jean was carrying a tray through the hall.

"Good morning, Dan. I thought we'd have breakfast on the porch." He was grateful that she didn't mention Sue's fall; that she acted as though it were any morning.

"Good, I'll take the tray out for you."

Unaccountably his spirits rose. He set the tray down on the table and stepped outside the door. The fresh feeling of the October morning quickened his blood. The berries on the barberry hedge were freshly lacquered a rich Chinese red. The tulip tree had a new streak of yellow and the woodbine on the garage had turned flame-colored over night. He walked as far as the corner of the house to see whether the asters had been frosted in the night. He wanted to prolong this part of the morning. When he turned and walked rapidly back to the porch his heels came down firmly on the flagstones.

Jean was there at one side of the card table, her small head tipped a little so her face tilted toward him. Her hair was barred with light and shadow by the sun slipping through the slats of the porch lattice.

"Been over the estate?"

Dan nodded, watching her lift the coffee pot and fill his cup. Cruelly his brain noted her deftness. He began his breakfast in silence. It was cool out here; the sun only came as far as the red line on the striped cloth.

"Alice Hutchins asked me to help with the bridge tea for the new instructors' wives today," Jean said. "She wants you to drop over afterwards with Hutch."

"Sounds natural; Sue used to have that tea here."

"Alice told me that; that's why I thought I might go so I could come back and tell Sue about it. Will you go then?"

Dan hesitated. "Yes, for a minute anyway; then I'll bring you home."

"Another piece of toast, Dan?"

"One to eat with my egg, please." He reached for the toast and met Jean's eyes. Jean smiled.

"Jean, I talked with Stephen yesterday." Dan looked out through the screen door at the woodbine. The green leaves dyed flame color were as unreal as Stephen's words. Without looking back at Jean he shook his head. "This is just a remission."

It was very quiet on the porch. He could hear Jean catch her breath.

"Oh, Dan, she seemed better, until this morning, of course."

He only shook his head. When he spoke again his voice was altered, more matter of fact. "I'm going to invite my new instructors over sometime this week; ask them to bring their wives, too. Sue asked me about them the other day. I think she misses having people around and the young people won't remind her so much of her illness as the older friends do."

"I thought Stephen wanted the house very quiet," Jean demurred.

"But he forgets we never have had a quiet house. All summer it's been like a morgue. It's better for everything to go on as usual. Having the place kept so quiet is enough to make Sue worry about herself. Hello, Donnie."

Jean's little daughter was very like her, he thought carelessly. She had Jean's short auburn hair, but her eyes were gray. She was small for her age, a little too nervous. She came toward them solemnly, her bib still on.

He had always thought if he had ever had children they would be chubby youngsters living in their own world, a comfortable world of nursery rhymes and simple food and early bed-times. Donnie looked at the world out of too-wise eyes and was more at home with grown-ups than children. Protectively, Dan put out his arm and swung her up on his chair. Life had turned things upside down for Donnie, too.

"Donna, did you eat your cereal?" Jean asked reproachfully. Dan was always a little amused to hear Jean use that motherly tone of voice.

Donna kept her eyes fixed on Dan. "I didn't care for it this morning," she answered calmly.

"But, Donna, Mother told you . . ."

Donna dropped her head on Dan's shoulder. "Please talk about something so Jean'll forget about the cereal, Dan," she whispered in his ear.

"Rascal!" he whispered back.

"Dan, don't let her spoil your breakfast. Donna, run and play till we're through."

Donna slipped down, content to go now that the

cereal was forgotten. "Can I ride to school with you, Dan?" She paused, twisting one foot behind the other, her eyes on his face.

"All right," he laughed. "Be out in the car, young lady, so I won't have to wait for you."

"Dan, you spoil her," Jean murmured reproachfully.

He thought as he did so often that he and Jean were going through all the motions of domesticity, sitting here for breakfast together. It was pleasant. He wondered what he would do without Jean here. He put down his napkin and pushed back his chair.

"I'll run up and see Sue."

He went quickly through the house but even as he went he was aware of Jean smiling at him.

"Will you be home for lunch, Dan?" she called after him.

"No," he answered without thinking. He ran upstairs like a boy late for class.

Sue was bathed and through with breakfast now. She was sitting up in bed waiting for him.

"Sue, you look lovely," he said a trifle self-consciously because of Agnes' steps going down the hall. Then the self-consciousness left him. He stooped and kissed her.

"Your fall didn't hurt you?"

"No. Oh, Dan, I never see you any more except like this, when you're going some place." The voice was faintly querulous.

Sue had seemed so close to him when he lay by himself this morning, but now the old Sue was completely lost in this invalid whose hand moved jerkily up to catch hold of his coat, whose flesh was so rigid, whose words slurred into one another. It was unthinkable that this could be Sue.

"Sue, I'll have time this evening. I can spend the whole evening home. We'll read aloud."

Her eyes watched him wistfully. "Dan, I'm so sick of it. I get better so slowly." She turned her face into the pillow and cried. He patted her awkwardly.

All the helpful things he told patients escaped him with Sue. He thought bitterly of one of Stephen Ridley's pet quotations, summing up the whole mission of a doctor: "To cure sometimes, to relieve often, to comfort always." With Sue he couldn't do even the least part of it.

"Dr. Norton has a wonderful personality." "Dr. Norton, your patients always seem brighter after you've been to see them." Complimentary things people told him mocked at him. He had almost believed them once. Now he could only stand by his wife's bed silently, like any husband, defeated and bewildered by her illness. How he could feel for those husbands now! He was like any one of them who followed the doctor out into the hall to ask about his wife's condition, a certain hopeless patience and fear in his eyes.

"Oh, Dan."

"Never mind, Sue; I'll be back early."

When he came out of the house, Donna was already there on the front seat. "Hello, Magpie"; he tweaked her cap.

He let the car slide slowly down the driveway. On Willow Road he stepped on the accelerator. On either side, students hurried along, intent on such momentous things as getting to their classes on time. But the flow of life along the street had nothing to do with Sue or with him. University Avenue was just as he had known it for so many autumns. Like an endless frieze, students were raking the leaves on the lawn of his old literary fraternity. The announcement of the first football game of the season was posted on the big signboard at the corner of the campus. But other years he had felt himself a part of this small world; now he seemed only to look on.

"You aren't cross, are you, Dan?"

"No, Donnie, of course not; why?"

"Well, you're awful quiet."

He looked at her and found Jean's expressive face tilted toward him. "I was thinking about that cereal you didn't eat," he told her. He let her out in front of her school and then drove slowly over to the hospital. He was in no hurry to begin the day's work.

Just as he parked at the curb, a battered old coupe came alongside and the driver honked loudly and called from the car,

"Hello, Dr. Norton!"

"Well, Whitney!"

A young man climbed out over a suitcase to shake hands with him. His pleasure at seeing him was so plain it warmed Dan.

"Just getting in to town?"

"Just this minute; we've driven a hundred miles since breakfast. I want you to meet my wife, Dan."

Dan went over to the car and shook hands with the young, eager-eyed girl who held a baby in her arms.

"Elsa, this is Dr. Norton; and this is the son and heir, Dan." His formality broke down.

Dan smiled. "Well, when I saw you last, Peter, you were an irresponsible intern. Now you have a wife and child! It's good to have you back as one of my instructors."

"It's good to be back, sir."

"He had to show me the hospital right away, Dr. Norton, even before he took me to the apartment!" the girl said. Dan looked at her again quickly. She made him think of Sue; she was so alive and it was so clear that she shared Peter's excitement.

"Yes, and do you know what she said, Dan? 'Oh, that building with the arms held out like a scarecrow,'" he mimicked her.

"But it's jealousy, Dr. Norton, because I know he'd leave even my arms for those!"

They drove off laughing, but some of their hilarity stayed with Dan as he went into the hospital.

3

JEAN KELLER going to a faculty tea! Jean Keller going to pour and be decorative at one end of the tea table! Sue Norton's sister trying to fill Sue's place! Jean mocked at herself as she went up the walk to the Hutchins' house. She had always shunned boring things and this was a bore. She had used to tell Sue that she let herself be imposed upon and forced into a dull, domestic rut because she couldn't say no.

She could have begged off. She could always say, "I don't like to leave Sue." But she had said instead, "Thank you, I'd like to"; because doing the things that Sue used to do seemed to bring her nearer to Dan. Because Alice Hutchins had said, "Then Hutch will bring Dan and Stephen home afterwards."

She lifted the cunningly wrought iron knocker and let it fall against the oak door. The simple act did more than announce her arrival; it acknowledged what before she had kept hidden from herself.

"Oh, Jean, you're a dear to come early. Come right up," Mrs. Hutchins called over the stair-rail.

"Sue sent her love to you," Jean said, taking off her hat and coat. "She wanted awfully to come." But she spoke without thinking of Sue.

"Poor darling! I miss her like everything," Alice Hutchins said. Then, in a briefer tone, she added, "There are only four new wives; I wrote their names out. You know how I am about names. But there will be twenty-six counting all the wives of the medical department. I think the tallies and pads and pencils are over in that desk; you see to them, will you, Jean?"

Jean arranged tables and counted cards and later she stood at the door with Alice Hutchins and greeted the newcomers.

"Mrs. Keith . . ." she heard herself repeating to Alice Hutchins . . . "and Mrs. Whitney." Jean smiled gaily as she greeted them, making up a little for Alice Hutchins' solid matter-of-factness.

"Yes, isn't it! Fall is a lovely time in Woodstock; but wait till you see it in the spring!" She sounded as though she had always lived here. In the spring . . . by spring . . . Alice Hutchins' voice beside her broke in on her own thoughts.

"My dear, I'm so glad you could come. I've heard Dr. Hutchins speak so well of your husband." It was her stock greeting. She must have been giving teas and saying the same words at them for years, Jean thought. Sue must have been better at these affairs. And Sue would never have been bored. It was uncanny how she was coming to know Sue so much better living in the same situations Sue had known.

"That's the last of them, Jean. I've counted twenty-four and you and I make twenty-six," Alice Hutchins said. "You pass the tallies and get them settled, dear; I want to see whether the cakes came."

When the women were all seated at the tables, Jean stood looking around the room. Of all these women she was the only one here who was not the wife of a doctor. The idea amused her. They did all have some common quality that marked them off in spite of their separate individualities. Perhaps it was pride, the fierce defensive pride of the wife of the ophthalmology man, always trying to push her husband beyond mediocrity, or the reluctant, sarcastic pride of Stella Ridley for Stephen. Their pride made them smug but happy, too. A woman wore her pride in her husband as she wore her furs, or her jewels. Without it any of these women, even Alice Hutchins, would be plain enough.

"John's been so busy lately, aside from his hospital work; you know, the patients that won't go to anyone else," the wife of the ophthalmology man was saying. Jean moved out of earshot, across to the table in the corner.

She watched the little pasteboards fall and smiled brightly at Elsa Whitney, but her mind was busy with one thought that she had secreted behind her thinking all day, until now.

Did she imagine it or had Dan's eyes lingered on hers longer than usual this morning at breakfast, with some special meaning?

They had shared so much in this last year; how could it not mean something to Dan, too? Or did Dan never think of her except as Sue's sister? Did he realize that she had been here a whole year?

The last year had been like a piece out of time; measured off in happenings rather than months. It seemed longer than only last October that Dan had driven down to Baltimore to bring her back after her divorce.

"Come along home with us, Jean, and stay till you catch your breath," was all he had said about the whole sorry mess.

She had not cared where she went at first. She had been sick of people. But she had forgotten that there were men like Dan, who were interested, outside and beyond themselves, in the work they did; like Stephen Ridley who was Dan's close friend, like the young doctors who were always dropping in to see Dan and Sue. Dan and Sue and their friends knew nothing about hate or self-pity or miserable living in cramped, squalid quarters. It had been easy to catch her breath here.

It had been easy to find herself loving Dan. Perhaps she had been in love with him in her teens when Sue first knew him. But this year had brought them together. How could it have been otherwise?

Someone laughed, a woman's high laugh of triumph. "There, and that trick's mine; I made it!"

Jean separated herself scornfully from these women and their pride and their talk. She glanced at plump little Mrs. Gailbraith still crowing over her grand slam, and then back to Prudence Keith, who was one of the new wives.

A voice carried back to Jean; just a phrase, "Mrs. Norton's sister . . . she's divorced and she keeps house . . ." She should be used to comments by this time, but she could feel the color rise in her neck. She busied herself about the room, saying the right word, emptying ash trays, advising nervous Mrs. Oakwood what to bid on her hand.

Little sentences isolated themselves from the monotonous murmur and rose above the ripples: "Do you like it here in Woodstock?" the wife of the heart man was asking Sylvia Kaplan, the pretty young Jewess whose husband was doing some special research work for Dan. "Of course you do," the voice went on. "A university town is delightful. I often tell Val I'd rather live here than any place I know."

Jean smiled at the self-congratulatory note she had heard so many times here in Woodstock.

"Have you any children, Mrs. Keith?" That was another familiar question. "Most of the young medical people have. I think it's rather fine. Rob was saying the other night, 'Where can you find a more normal group than right here?' It keeps us young to live among them."

Jean's mind writhed away from the fatuousness of this remark. Couldn't they see that each year's new group of young people measured against themselves only made them seem older? Not all the young people in the University could keep Dan's youth for him if he were to go on the way he had been. Sue's illness was going to make him resigned and old before his time.

Alice Hutchins raised her eyebrows comically at her

from the door. This was the last hand. Jean went about the room gathering up the tallies.

There was no more tea to pour just now. Stella Ridley helped herself to another cucumber sandwich. She always came to the first medical bridge of the year and always poured because Stephen Ridley was head of the research department. Sue Norton had always poured at the other end of the long table where Jean Keller sat today.

After the first bridge Stella hardly ever bothered to come and wives with lesser ratings presided. By spring the honor might even descend to the wife of one of the assistant professors.

But she always enjoyed the first bridge. It was interesting to see the new wives. They were always alike in a way, eager young things so set on being the perfect wives to their doctor husbands. Sometimes they had been nurses, sometimes debutantes or spry young things who kept talking about the jobs they used to have.

But wait until their husbands couldn't get away to go places, or came home too tired to bother to dress and go out, or talked medicine all through one of their most carefully planned dinners, then some of that bright young assurance would go. They would learn to go their own way or give up and come to live in their gardens or their children.

A great deal depended on their husbands, of course. But now they were all deeply in love; they always were. There was something romantic about doctors when you were young.

Then Stella Ridley's sharp glance switched to Jean Keller across the table from her. She felt a certain prejudice against this sister of Sue Norton's because of the fondness she felt for Sue.

She had seen so many familiar figures in the close little world of the faculty medical school drop out. You couldn't live in a place for twenty years without that happening, but no death nor moving away, nor illness had shaken the whole pleasant fabric of their living as had Sue Norton's invalidism. And now Sue seemed willingly to have dropped off all connection with her old friends. Her face that was so subtly altered smiled back at you when you talked until the spiciest bits of gossip you had saved to tell her seemed too trivial to mention. It had been almost a relief when Stephen said he thought Dan would rather not have Sue's old friends call for a while, it seemed to upset Sue so.

"Nice group, Stella." Alice Hutchins broke in on her thoughts.

"Yes, poor things; isn't it a much smaller group than usual?"

"Yes, Hutch said the department just doesn't know where it stands financially this year. The regents blame it on the legislature, of course, and do nothing. He just had to cut down."

"I miss Sue Norton at these things, Alice; it seems queer not to have her at the table pouring."

Alice Hutchins shook her head. "I know it, Stella. I can't get used to the idea of Sue's being an invalid. Hutch says it's hard on Dan's work, too."

Both women were silent. Alice Hutchins' face was less stolid, touched by sadness. Stella Ridley set her lips grimly.

"I asked Jean about her today and she said there wasn't much change. She says she sits without saying a word for an hour at a time and you know that isn't like her."

"You know Sue and Dan always did so much for the young people on the staff. I used to feel guilty, but Hutch and I are always so busy . . ." Mrs. Hutchins' voice trailed off into silence.

"I imagine the Nortons will be pretty quiet this year," Stella said.

At the other end of the long table Jean was aware that Stella Ridley and Alice Hutchins were talking about Sue. She recognized the air of sadness about their voices and their faces. Everywhere she went people asked her about Sue in just such a tone of voice.

They felt so badly for Sue that they scarcely thought of Dan. They never seemed to think what a burden Sue's illness was to him, or that he was never free from illness. It was a tragedy for Sue, of course, but it was more of a tragedy for Dan to be dragged, living and well, along with her.

She was not sure that the last year had not been easier than this year when Sue was a little better.

Last fall, Sue's illness had come on them so suddenly! She had meant to go to New York and find a job, any kind of a job, when she came, but she had given that up, seeing how much she could do here. Dan was worried, abstracted. Sue had been in the hospital for three weeks and Dan had stayed right there most of the time. Dan had scarcely seemed aware of her presence in the house.

Friends of Sue's came often to ask how she was in those first months. There had been flowers and notes to write to thank their donors.

"I am writing for my sister, Mrs. Norton, to thank you . . ." "Sue has asked me . . ." "Dr. Norton has asked me to express his appreciation . . ."

She had refused all invitations at first. "Thank you, but I couldn't just now until we see . . ."

It had been easy to live in the fierce heat of a crisis. She had not thought of herself then. Anything in the world she could do for Sue, she would do so gladly.

But slowly the crisis had passed. The tension eased.

Sue was better, or not really better; Dan said there was a remission in the disease; a cold word, neither well nor worse, simply a little breathing space. It was like falling down a cliff and catching hold of a bush, stopping your fall, hanging there to look both ways, up again and down. They were all hanging there; although Sue, of course, didn't know it.

Now that Sue was better it was more difficult to make her feel she was progressing. She had moods; she was more irritable. She tried to do things beyond her strength, as she had this morning. . . .

"It's been so nice to see you again, Mrs. Keller."

"Good-by, Mrs. Keller. . . ."

Jean smiled and murmured something, wondering how long she had been staring into space.

When the last of the "medical wives" had left, Alice Hutchins sank down wearily on the couch.

"Well, that's over!"

Stella Ridley fished a compact someone had left out of the big wing chair and settled herself comfortably. Jean Keller drew up another chair so the three women made a little circle in the middle of the room. Around them the deserted bridge tables were still strewn with cards and score-pads, scrawled with sums like the pages of small girls' arithmetic books.

"That Elsa Whitney is attractive," Jean commented.

"Yes, but they're all sort of pathetic," Stella remarked. "They come here so thrilled it sticks out all over them and you know how it will be; their husbands will either be so absorbed in their work that they'll have no time for them, or so politic and business-like or so completely mediocre that they'll lose their halos. The whole thing is a sad business."

"Why, Stella, you're positively jaundiced!" Alice Hutchins said reproachfully.

Stella Ridley looked out the long windows into the Hutchins' garden. It was bare now with the rose bushes wrapped in burlap and the garden furniture all moved in. What would they do, she and Alice, without their gardens and homes!

"Alice, may I take Sue a plate of canapés?" Jean asked. "They were so pretty."

"Canapés are awful when they've stood a while." Alice Hutchins twisted her mouth in disgust.

"I wouldn't wonder if that's the way the reports of things she hasn't been to and the tid-bits of gossip seem to Sue," Stella observed tartly.

"Well, resting from your labors?" Dr. Hutchins and Dan Norton stood in the doorway.

Dr. Hutchins was all that could be asked for in a picture of the successful professional man: more impressive than Dan Norton, but a little too much on the suave side. He had made a name for himself with a monograph on ulcers of the stomach, but that was some time ago and the activities of the school had crowded out his clinical work.

Stella Ridley's glance turned to Dan Norton as he stood talking to Mrs. Hutchins. He looked tired tonight. He had never fitted into her classifications for medical husbands. He was absorbed in his work and yet he and Sue had never grown apart. The Nortons were a by-word for devotion.

One of the virtues of their academic world was their

ability to keep their personal sorrows well concealed. Here they all were stiffly avoiding the mention of Sue, and yet they must all be thinking, as she was, how queer it was not to have Sue here with Dan. Why didn't they ever say what they thought, simply and freely? Why didn't she say now, "I miss Sue, Dan."

"Dan, are your new instructors as young and eager as this parcel of wives we've been feeding tea to?" she asked instead.

"The new crop isn't bad," Dan said, smiling, but with a preoccupation that seemed so strange in him it hurt her.

Stella Ridley struck a match sharply.

4

PETER, we mustn't stay long over here because I told Mrs. Janowski we were just going to make a call. She gets 35 cents an hour for staying with children!"

"Sure," Peter answered absent-mindedly. He was driving slowly, looking at the winding streets that turned off to the left. "I haven't been here, of course, since Dan had a bunch of us over for beer the summer I was an intern. It's a big brown house about a mile back on one of these streets.

"Woodstock is lovely," Elsa said, waving her hand vaguely at the street in front of them, at the lawns sloping back from the curb, the low-hanging arches of the yellow elms.

"Mmm," Peter agreed out of his deep content in being back. "When I was here before I was always missing you."

Elsa squeezed his knee.

"That's the house!" Peter nodded ahead at a big brown, cupola-topped house at the head of a steep drive.

"What a funny, old-fashioned place, Peter!"

"That's Dan!" Peter explained. "Most of the faculty big-wigs, Madame, feel that they must live in a certain place, in a house that does 'em credit, and have everything as good as the next head of a department. But good old Dan sees a place with trees and a view so he gets it, fashionable or not. Maybe his wife had something to do with it. A man's wife is important," he added, looking sidewise at Elsa.

"Oh?" Elsa answered. "I didn't know that."

"Oh, yes, very important to a doctor."

Elsa chewed her lip meditatively. "Too bad you didn't take longer in making your choice, Dr. Whitney."

"I know, but I was a rash young man." Peter turned the car into the drive. "Isn't this a grand place for a mob of people?"

"Do they have children, Peter?"

"Nope, just Mrs. Norton and Dan. She's a lovely

person; I used to think of you when I'd see her out here or waiting for Dan in front of the hospital."

There were four cars parked along the drive as they came up. Lights streamed out through the tangled creepers that covered one side of the house. The front door was open.

"Peter, are you sure it isn't a party?"

"Oh, no, Dan just likes people around. Everyone is always dropping in."

Jean met them at the door. "Hello, we've been looking for you. Take your coat upstairs, Mrs. Whitney." The warmth in her voice, like the warmth of the house, drew them into an intimate circle.

Peter found Dan sitting in his big chair by the fire. He was leaning forward, listening to something one of the boys was saying.

"Glad to see you, Peter!" he called out. "Kaplan's just been trying to draw me out on the subject of State medicine; very subtly though." Dan laughed as the young man reddened slowly. "Well, I'll tell you, Kaplan, I think it's the right idea without any question, but I'm not sure that I as an individual shall like it. It will certainly change the whole medical picture. What was the feeling about it in the East, Peter?"

There was a glint of curiosity in Dan's eyes as he listened to Peter. Peter was the one who had written at the end of a clear account of a certain treatment, "but I think I'll live to see this treatment abandoned." Dan had liked that. He had urged Hutchins to get Peter back here this year. They must keep an eye on him.

Dan left everything to Jean. She saw that there was beer for everyone, and cigarettes; that everyone had met everyone else as Sue used to do. He settled back in his chair. He filled his pipe and passed the big bowl of tobacco over to Keith.

After the quiet of the last few months this was good. These youngsters were a relief from the solicitous heaviness of his own contemporaries. He wanted to see these new men out of their white coats, to see their wives; to talk with them and smoke with them and drink with them. That was the only way to know what they were like; or was it that he wanted to forget his own worries for a while, letting himself be drawn out by their lives and problems? His mind slid away from that reasoning.

He looked around with satisfaction. Tom Barton was the husband of Sue's nurse. She had been nursing for years to put him through medical school. Tom was a good plodding sort, nothing brilliant. Perhaps he had kept Tom on here because of Agnes.

Keith and Kaplan were new to Woodstock. Kaplan was one of those sensitive young Jews who made up for a car-load of the run-of-the-mill sort.

There was a certain tension about Keith; he'd noticed that on the ward yesterday. Good personality, a little turned in on itself. Queer, how that sort usually had a wife as fine-drawn and high-strung as himself! Jean said Keith's wife was the daughter of some professor at Harvard. Her accent now cut across Agnes Barton's Middle Western voice with devastating clearness. Those two girls wouldn't have any more in common than their husbands would.

"Dr. Norton, wasn't it Cass in Boston who wrote that article on water balance?" Keith called out.

As Elsa came out of the front bedroom into the upper hall, the sound of Dr. Norton's laugh rose above the other laughter and voices. Music from the victrola or radio ran an undertone. It sounded like a great many people having a very good time. Elsa hesitated at the head of the stairs, savoring the sounds. This was what Peter meant when he had talked about the fun of living in Woodstock.

"Jean says I don't have to!" a child's voice, sure of itself, a little petulant, came clearly down the hall.

"But it's late, Donna, hurry and pop into bed or I'll have to call Agnes." The adult's voice was curiously toneless, some of the words slurred.

"Agnes is downstairs, too," the child's voice triumphed. "I'm going downstairs and see the party!"

There was a brief silence in which Elsa could feel the exasperation of the older person. Impulsively, she went toward the voices. She stopped short in the doorway.

"Oh, I beg your pardon, I thought . . ."

Sue Norton smiled back at Elsa, seeing in her face her surprise at the hospital bed.

"Come in." Sue's voice was slow, painstakingly precise.

"I'm Elsa Whitney; I thought perhaps I could help."

"Aunt Sue is trying to chase me to bed," the child offered.

"I'm Sue Norton." Sue half started to reach out her hand and then didn't for fear her arm would jerk suddenly. She saw the girl's hand move and then fall back on the watch on her other wrist. "You're new here, aren't you?" The girl's embarrassment made Sue feel more at ease.

"Yes, we've only been here a week."

"I remember a young Dr. Whitney . . . he was a student here."

"That was Peter," Elsa said eagerly. "He's thrilled to be back here with Dr. Norton this year." She turned to the child. "Can I tuck you in bed now?"

Donna had climbed over the end of the hospital bed and perched there watching Elsa. She shook her head.

"I'm going downstairs first and see everyone and then Dan'll bring me up pick-a-back." She jumped down from the bed and ran around Elsa toward the door. Elsa glanced at Sue.

"Never mind; we haven't had anyone here at the house for a long time and Donna can't bear to miss seeing them. I . . . I've been ill," she added. She was pleased that her words came out so clearly this time; that she wasn't uncomfortable with this girl. When Dan had suggested bringing some of them in to meet her, or taking her downstairs she had said, "Not yet, Dan," but this girl had come in of her own accord and she didn't mind her at all.

"We met Dr. Norton the morning we drove in to town," Elsa said. She must keep on talking. Speech seemed so difficult for Mrs. Norton. Peter had said she was lovely but that must have been before. Peter hadn't known she was sick. Her face seemed to have no expression in it; it was like the face of a very fat person, and yet it was not fat; it was almost gaunt.

". . . He must have thought us crazy; we had everything packed in the car with us and the baby." She felt herself speaking too loudly.

Sue smiled. Her eyes brightened. "When Dan came back to Woodstock as an instructor we had no car. He had his first suit of civilian clothes . . ." her tongue had trouble with the word civilian . . . "after the army. He looked so red and muscle . . . muscle-bound." But her words ran into laughter. Her amusement in the recollection was in her eyes. Elsa noticed now that they were brown.

Dan came in carrying Donna pick-a-back; bouncing

her up and down, tickling her bare feet until she was convulsed by giggles.

"Hello, Mrs. Whitney!" He let Donna slide down his back. "I see you and Mrs. Norton are already acquainted." Sue was laughing quite naturally. All the time he was in the other room tucking Donna back in bed, he strained to hear Sue's voice talking with Peter's wife, to hear her laugh like that again. He had been right; new people were what Sue needed, young people.

"Sing that song about 'Drink, drink,' Dan, or I won't stay in bed!" Donna called shrilly out through the door.

"Donna, keep quiet now or I'll come back and spank you!" he growled, but he felt like singing. The atmosphere of his house was natural again. Sue was more like herself. Perhaps, after all, they were going to go on living again.

" 'Drink, drink, joy rules the day
Who will have thoughts for the morrow . . .' "

he sang as he went back to Sue's room. He finished with a flourish, holding out an imaginary cup to Sue:

" 'So here's to your health, *lass*, and mine,
So here's to your health, *lass*, and mine!'

Want to change your mind and let me carry you downstairs for a while, Sue?"

"Not tonight, Dan." But she was smiling at him.

"You won't be lonely?"

"Not a bit."

"I'll be up again. Come on, Mrs. Whitney, and meet the rest of your husband's colleagues."

Dan sipped his beer and looked over the brim of his stein at all of them. He saw Agnes slip off upstairs to Sue's room. The boys were contrasting services at their different hospitals. Sylvia Kaplan and Jean and MacLean, the intern who had dropped in late, were down at the other end of the room by the radio.

He looked at Elsa Whitney and Prudence Keith sitting on the couch in front of the fire, Prue smoking her cigarette with an air of fastidious detachment; then back at their husbands assuming unconsciously in their talk that they represented the best in medical wisdom. Dan felt an urge to shake their young assurance.

He turned to Elsa and Prue. "You know, you girls feel that there's something about the profession that constitutes a certain security from, oh, we'll say, the stodginess of the ordinary business man. You girls see yourselves living your lives in a rarefied atmosphere because you married doctors, isn't that so?"

In spite of the joking way he had started out, a certain intensity had crept into Dan's voice and they were all listening.

"But you want to remember that there's nothing in our profession to guarantee that your husbands won't grow stodgy and complacent or even as ignorant and unscrupulous as quacks. I've seen it happen. These years here they're safe enough; these years are all eagerness and earnestness.

"You boys think by your extra training here, by your unusual qualities of mind, your love for each other, that you're secure from failure and mediocrity. But this is only an interval. The world will reach out with its slow contagion. . . ."

"Dan, darling, don't be so gloomy! You'll scare these babes!" Jean exclaimed.

He laughed. "That was quite an oration. I was just teasing them, Jean. Have another round of beer while I go up and say good night to Mrs. Norton."

When they came out of the Nortons' Elsa and Peter drove silently for a block.

Was it as Dr. Norton said that after their living here the world would change them, catch them in "its slow contagion," or had he just been talking? Elsa wondered.

"Peter, tell me about Mrs. Norton. I heard that little girl, I guess she's Mrs. Keller's child, and I went down the hall and there was Mrs. Norton. She's in a hospital bed, Peter!"

"I know; Barton was telling me about her. His wife is her nurse. Mrs. Norton has multiple sclerosis, mainly a spinal cord disease. I understand they began to suspect it about a year ago. She'll never get well, of course." Peter drove quietly, then he burst out, "It's a horrible thing! You can see what a strain Dan's under. Think of a blow like that falling on him when he's right at the top of his profession!"

Elsa saw Sue Norton's face that was expressionless until she smiled. She heard her queer, toneless voice. She thought of her off upstairs while they were all downstairs. She shivered suddenly, feeling the cold fall night for the first time. Then, swiftly, she escaped back to the warm present of their own lives.

"We'll have to pay Mrs. Janowski for six hours. We left home at quarter of seven, Peter!"

"All right, it was worth it," Peter said.

5

THE lights came through the bare branches of the trees on campus, showing up their angular grotesqueries. Dry leaves blew against the steps of the Science building and rattled noisily along the walk, crackling under the feet of an occasional passer-by. Across through the trees the lights in Academy Hall emblazoned the great leaded glass windows two hours before the hall would fill for the first symphony concert of the year.

The street light on the corner touched but dimly on Jean sitting back in the seat of the car. It left Dan's face in shadow. They had been sitting there for half an hour, scarcely speaking.

"Dan, we must go; we were invited for six-thirty and Stella likes people on time," Jean said.

Dan took out another cigarette and lighted it.

"Come, Dan." Jean put her hand on his arm.

"Do you think Sue would go to the concert if I went back and urged her?"

"She loves music, of course," Jean said faintly, "but I think she dreads having people stare at her now. You know she was worse after that one time last winter."

Jean pulled on her long white gloves, working them down on her fingers. Now that Sue had said no and Dan had agreed that he thought she better wait she hoped he wouldn't decide to try it anyway and go back for Sue after Stella's dinner. It was so conspicuous. They had to go so slowly down the aisle of the auditorium, Dan's arm around Sue. She would help Sue on the other side, conscious of the whisperings that followed them: "That's Mrs. Norton's sister . . . she runs his house. . . ." An eyebrow raised here and there. "Quite a situation, isn't it?"

Someone ran across the campus and the dry leaves whispered sharply under foot, like two women gossiping.

"She didn't seem to mind too much, did she?" Dan asked.

"No, she looked very cozy when we left, and then she has the radio. They broadcast the concert, you know."

"I'm too tired to go any place for dinner tonight," Dan said almost petulantly.

"I know, Dan; if we'd called up sooner, but now they'll be waiting for us."

Dan put on his hat and started the car with a jerk.

"Dan, it hurts me to see you so tired and harassed." Jean spoke very softly. She waited for him to speak. If he would just say one word to show . . .

"We're not late; there's Hutch going up the walk now," he said instead.

In the Academy the lights were already dimming when the Ridleys, the Hutchins and Dan and Jean arrived. The student ushers gave them their programs and hurried up the aisles. The musicians were already on the stage, tuning their instruments. The swish and rustle and bustle of a thousand people settling themselves had quieted.

From the quick staccato tap of the conductor's baton expectant silence flowed over the audience. The music came. It poured out over the people, drawing them all together, yet freeing them within the privacy of that volume of sound.

Stella Ridley glanced at her husband, knowing how he would look: his fine wrinkled face was alert in listening and she saw the special small pleased smile he had for perfect execution, either of a laboratory experiment or a cello's part. Now his fingers on his knee moved slightly, marking the rhythm. When he went home he would say, his voice somehow cutting in across the glow she had brought home from the concert, "Stella, undoubtedly, the Philadelphia gives a more brilliant performance. The first violins were better tonight, though, in the second movement, don't you think?" And her glow would fade under the effect of his analysis.

"I don't know, but I loved it tonight," she would say.

And he would answer, "You lose half of it, Stella, unless you listen with your mind, too."

Stephen glanced over at her. She nodded. He wanted her to notice the harp coming in there. She watched the woman over at the corner of the stage, half hidden by her harp, sitting so still, waiting for the moment when she should pluck her few notes. She was like that harpist, plucking her few notes in Stephen's life. She smiled back at him as the harpist lifted her hands ever so softly from the strings. Stephen loved the harp.

Mrs. Hutchins sat very straight. She remembered to hold her head back so the muscles of her throat pulled taut. The woman in the beauty parlor had said, "When you're at a concert or lecture or in church give a thought to your face." Surreptitiously she smoothed her neck down to the low V of her gown. She wondered if Dan had looked at Sue's sister in a—oh, a special way—tonight at dinner.

In an interval that was suddenly so empty after the

music, people shifted in their seats. Mrs. Hutchins nudged Dr. Hutchins. The doctor sighed, opened his eyes slowly while the corners of his mouth pulled down. He consulted his program minutely. It was his way of waking in a public place; it gave the impression that he had been lost in contemplation.

Dan sat at the end of the row. He closed his eyes as the music began again and let it surround him. He was so quiet Jean wondered if he were asleep, but even in the half-dark she could see the movement of the little muscle in his cheek. At the Ridleys' he had been so gay at dinner he had set them all laughing. The mood he had had in the car he seemed to have thrown off completely. On the way back to the Academy he hadn't mentioned going home for Sue. She glanced over at him again.

When he opened his eyes suddenly she felt herself caught unawares, as though her love must show in her face. She swallowed, hearing the sound loudly. Thc music came to a close on a small note that hung in the silence like the sound of a coin dropped in a quiet church. They were together in that intimate silence. Dan must feel it too.

People were clapping all around them, but Dan's hands were still. His eyes still held hers. Then as the conductor turned toward the orchestra Dan clapped. Jean lifted her hands and clapped too, but hers were cold and moist.

The stage became a shambles. The orchestra, through with their smiling and bowing, broke up like a town-meeting, and left a confusion of rickety chairs and angular music-racks behind. Light that was harsh after the mellow half shadow flooded the Academy. The aisles became a fashion parade.

"Shall we go out, Jean?" Dan asked. Jean glanced at Stella Ridley and Alice Hutchins preparing to stay while their husbands went out for a smoke and knew she would have to move over and sit with them.

"Yes, let's go all the way out and get some air."

The lobby was crowded with people Dan knew; people they both knew. They stopped to talk with a group at the door. Jean was introduced to a friend of Sue's who had been in Europe for the last year.

"I heard Sue's sister was here, of course; I'm so glad to meet you. How is Sue?"

Jean pressed Dan's arm to remind him that they were going out, and slipped into the wrap he held for her.

Out on the broad steps in front of the Academy mostly students gathered. The mingled sound of their voices was a young sound, filtered through laughter.

"Look, Dan!" They laughed at a co-ed in a scarlet cape who held three youths enthralled. From a group of students who scorned the affectation of dressing for a concert and came in sweaters with mops of uncombed hair they heard scraps of conversation interlarded with Marxist quotations. Dan chuckled.

Jean pointed out a Chinese girl in native costume walking with a Chinese youth in tweeds.

They met the Whitneys, walking arm in arm around the half block from one entrance to the other.

"We've just been congratulating ourselves that we came back here instead of going into practice this year," Peter said, "even if it takes our last nickel."

"We might have been trying to get this concert on the radio! Isn't it heavenly?" Elsa's face glowed. "It makes you feel so alive!"

From inside the sound of a bugle came faintly. The crowds moved toward the doors.

"Come on, burbler," Peter said, "we'll have to hump if we're going to make it; we're up three flights!"

"I like to see those two," Dan said. "He'll get somewhere with her to help."

"Dan, you're so fatherly about your instructors!" There was a hint of annoyance in her light tone. "But you've been more like yourself, tonight," she said, trying to bring Dan back to themselves. It was almost as though Elsa's shining young face had come between them.

As they slipped into their seats, the full, waiting hush had already fallen. The sound of Jean's wrap as Dan laid it back against the seat seemed loud.

The conductor appeared. Applause crackled against the hush, swept to a peak, and lumbered away like horses' hoofs crossing a covered bridge.

Dan shrugged into a more comfortable position in his seat. His eyes sought the ledge of the balcony where the brass railing flowed in a liquid stream through the darkness. Now the sweep of the music that had soothed him before the intermission failed him. He was cast back on his own thoughts.

He should have brought Sue. It would have been more difficult this year, but it was such a little thing to do. Perhaps Sue had said no, thinking of him. Even if she did shy at the thought of people looking at her, he mustn't encourage her in that. After the Ridleys' dinner it had been too late to go back for her. He had let himself believe her when she said she was better off at home listening to the concert over the radio.

He missed talking with her in the old way. Perhaps her thinking was the same; it was hard to be sure. He remembered as a little boy reaching for bright pebbles in the brook, but when he got them out in his hand they were just like any dull stones. That was the way Sue's thoughts, put in her poor slurred speech, lost all their color. They almost ceased to be Sue's.

The high, piercing note of the oboe penetrated his thoughts, insistent, mercilessly sweet, vibrating whatever truth there was in him. Well, then, he had wanted to come to this concert without Sue; to shake off for one night the strain, the weight of Sue's affliction; not to be kind, thoughtful, a figure in the little faculty world to be pointed out . . . "there's Dan Norton with his wife, you know . . . tragic thing . . ." Just this once, to go as he had used to, with Sue; with Jean this time, to a concert.

Jean barely touched his sleeve. He met her eyes. "Perfect!" she breathed, scarcely whispering it.

He nodded, thankful as the unbearable note of the oboe ended. Now the music was more earthy; there was the theme again.

It was a relief to be with Jean. Why should he feel half guilty about it? He had looked forward to it all evening. When he had caught her eyes during the music, it had been like some moment with Sue. But Jean was different. She made him feel as though they had each come a long way, but now they were together. Perhaps it was because of the bitterness of Jean's married life, perhaps the last year that they had been through together.

He pulled his program out of his pocket. There were still two more numbers. He leaned over to Jean. She had not been clapping, only sitting; quiet, lovely.

"Let's go home to Sue," he murmured, trying not to look straight into her eyes. Jean seized her wrap and was already standing. They moved swiftly up the aisle. They reached the doors at the back before the applause had ended. In the lobby he held her cape for her. "Do you mind too much?"

"Not a bit, I was getting sleepy," Jean lied.

"You wait here and I'll bring the car around."

"No, I'll go with you, the air feels good."

He took her arm and they went out into the night just as the music began, like some far-off sound of unattainable joy. They walked in silence to the rear of the Science building where the car was parked. Jean glanced at him quickly and then looked away, down the darkened streets of the town.

"I'm afraid Sue will be asleep by now, anyway," she said and wished the words unsaid. The simple statement had turned the unacknowledged intimacy of the evening into something guilty. All the music faded out of her brain as though it had never been. Dan was driving fast; why did he drive so fast?

Agnes lit the gas fire in Mrs. Norton's room and turned the dial of the radio for the concert.

"There, now are you comfortable, Mrs. Norton? The concert should begin in a few minutes."

"I think I'll move into a chair instead of lying on the couch. I can manage alone, I think."

Sue pulled herself up by the end of the couch. The table was next to it, then Dan's chair. "I'm getting so much better," Sue said.

"Yes, indeed," Agnes agreed.

"I should really have gone tonight. Dr. Norton wanted to come back for me," Sue said slowly.

Agnes watched her let herself down stiffly in the big

chair. Mrs. Norton was pretty in the black negligee, even with her face so changed.

Agnes took her knitting and sat across from her.

"It's good to feel better," Sue said. She reached out to the table for a book and the jerking of her hand made the whole table shake.

"Did you ever have a case like mine before, Agnes?" Sue asked suddenly.

"No, it just happens that I never have, Mrs. Norton," Agnes answered quickly.

"I just wondered how soon I can hope for improvement in my hands. Dr. Norton says it will be slow."

Agnes was relieved when she went back to her book. When the music began she put her book back on the table. "It isn't the same not seeing the people come in or moving around with them in the intermission. Will you turn off the lights, please."

Agnes was glad she had her knitting. Just sitting in a room with only the fire and the music and with Mrs. Norton sitting with her eyes closed, not saying anything, made her feel sad. Poor dear, asking how long it would be before her arms and legs were better! Agnes pulled her yarn a little looser. She was knitting faster and faster, keeping up with the music. The music ended. The applause over the radio sounded farther off than the music had. Mrs. Norton sighed.

Agnes laid down her knitting. "Would you mind if I went down to call Tom a minute, Mrs. Norton?"

Sue shook her head. She must ask Agnes about Tom.

She had been so wrapped up in her own troubles. She had not used to be like that. She thought back over the long year behind her. It was over now and she was better; she mustn't slip back into that feeling that nothing mattered. And even if, even while, her legs kept so stiff and her hands jerked, the rest of her living could go on just as it always had. She must do all she could.

The music swept her along with it and gave her strength. Now while Agnes was gone she got to her feet with difficulty and practiced walking the length of the room. She was stronger than she had been the other morning. The music rose, carrying her above the lonely feeling she had had ever since Dan and Jean left for dinner. The music was triumphant. Nothing mattered now that she was improving. She mustn't let herself mind being left home alone. She reached the mantel and stood leaning against it. The low heat from the gas flames was comforting against her legs.

"Why, Mrs. Norton!" Agnes' surprise was plain on her face. "Don't . . . you won't tire yourself, will you?"

"No. I've been lying down too long." Her legs felt shaky in spite of their curious rigidity, as though they didn't belong to her. But it was so good to stand up. She looked at her shadow cast along the ceiling.

"Was—was Tom home?" she asked.

"Yes, I wanted him to go, but he wouldn't without me. He said he couldn't enjoy it if I weren't there.

. . ." Agnes stopped, confused. "He isn't naturally musical, I mean," she said quickly.

But Sue had noticed. Dan used to reach out for her hand under cover of her coat when the music was something they both loved. Did he miss her by him at the concert? It was only half hearing it like this. It must be only half hearing it for Dan.

A high, clear note of the oboe rose above the violins, unearthly, lonely, thin, but so sweet! A fuller note could not have reached so high. It rose above niggardliness of spirit, above hurt. It made her content.

During the applause that came over the radio she moved back to the chair. She was glad to have Agnes help her. Her body that was hardly hers was grateful to sit down. The couch would have felt better, but she wouldn't let herself tonight.

"Next time I must ask Dan to get a program before the concert. I think next time I'll feel equal to going," she added.

The front door clicked. Jean and Dan were home already, before the concert was over! Excitement throbbed in her mind, shouldering the content aside. Her eyes held excitement. They were as eager as any child's. There was Dan coming upstairs.

"Quick, Agnes, help me up." She must meet him standing.

"Dear, I came home to hear the rest of the concert with you. Why, Sue!" He lifted her in his arms and laid her down on the couch. His face against hers was cold. His clothes held the smell of fresh air. He sat down beside her and pulled a program out of his pocket. The concert still came clearly over the radio but she wasn't listening.

Happiness warmed her. Happiness was so different from her painfully achieved content.

6

HOW about a little work tonight?" Dan asked when he came upstairs after dinner. He had an armful of books with yellow paper markers protruding from their pages and a folder bulging with proof sheets.

Sue smiled. The room that had been small all day was large enough. The gas fire was as merry as any wood fire.

Dan came back whistling. He brought a card-table and set it up in front of the Morris chair and moved all his books over on it.

"This bedside table of yours will be fine. We should have had one of these before, Sue."

Instantly the angular one-legged table lost its hospital stamp and became a respectable piece of furniture.

"Now . . ." Dan began. "Well, let's wait till I get my pipe filled."

It was like the old days. She had watched him so many times before she knew every gesture; how his fingers would tamp down the tobacco in the bowl, how his cheeks would suck in at the mouth, how he would hunt for a match.

"When we get through we'll have apples. Remember we always used to."

"I haven't eaten an apple for so long." Her sentence came to an end without any inflection of her voice to mark a period.

Dan took infinite time arranging his papers and books.

"You're wasting time," she said.

"Always did; I'm all right when I get started."

"What's the paper on?"

He told her. "I want you to read the proof sheets; they're full of mistakes. They couldn't read the notes I put in after it was typed."

"That's funny," Sue said ponderously.

He glanced at her in humorous rebuke. It was all just as it used to be, or almost.

"Now, if you'll do these first ten pages, dear, for typographical errors." He laid the sheets over the table. The paper was shiny under her hand. The type had a moist look. She started reading. The words meant very little, but that was a help in proofreading, because the meaning didn't beguile her over misspellings.

"In hypoparathyroidism, htere is a reduction of the . . ."

The t and the h were reversed. She moved the pencil down to the page, holding it under her hand rather than between her thumb and finger. She made the mark without thinking about it and her hand obeyed. The line she drew scrawled.

She went on reading. The room was very quiet. Only the breathing sound of the gas flame, an occasional puff from Dan's pipe, the shuffle of his pages.

"Mhmmm!" he said to himself, banging a reference book shut.

"Is this word spelled right?" she asked aloud.—"Dan?"

"What?" Dan asked slowly. He was deep in his own page. Then she laughed. He was always slow to come out of his own reading. "Dan!"

He came over to see what she meant. "My secretaries don't shout at me," he told her. They were back where they had always been.

There was a word misspelled. She pounced on it. She tried to change the letter, but she couldn't make her pencil move in so small a space. She drew a line so Dan would see the place.

"Let me read you what Tinturn says, Sue."

Sue leaned her head back to listen. Her hand shook from holding the pencil. It bothered her that such a little thing could tire her so. She had worked for hours on papers of Dan's, typing and correcting them. They had sat up till all hours. And now at nine o'clock, when they had barely begun she felt so tired. But it was only that she was out of practice.

Dan's voice stopped. She hadn't heard a word. She made a sound in her throat of approval. She had not used to do that. She used to be able to follow a medical article.

She picked up her pencil and tried again, following the lines across. Quotation marks were omitted. She held the proof sheet with her arm. She tried so hard the tremor was worse.

"Dan, will my hands get so I can ever really write with them? I'm so much better and my hands keep right on shaking."

Dan looked up at her. His mind was still on what he had been reading.

"What, Sue? I was right in the middle of a bit here by Tinturn."

It wasn't what he said. It was the irritation in his voice. She knew he wasn't even thinking of her, but she felt her eyes fill with tears. A tear dropped wetly on her hand. She wouldn't lift her hand to wipe her eyes lest Dan should notice. He didn't have to answer like that!

"Here's this part I was looking for, Sue; I'll read it to you."

Dan hadn't even known he was answering crossly. She should know Dan. She tried to concentrate on each word as he read it.

"I could quote that in there if you think it would make it any clearer? See, it would go in there on that page you have there." Dan came over to show her.

Sue lifted the long sheet clumsily. Her corrections were vague lines such as a child might make. They scrawled across the page. He remembered how neatly she used to correct the proof sheets of his papers. He had not realized the tremor had increased so. He started to go over to his table. Sue lay back against her pillow and looked up at him. He saw she had been crying.

"We'll stop for now, Sue. You mustn't try to do too much the first time."

"The apples, Dan."

"Oh, yes; I'll go get them." Dan folded the proof sheets and piled up the books. He folded up the table with as much noise as he could. "I've been asked to do quite an extensive article for the *Maryland Research Journal* for June so I want to get this out of the way. Thank you, Sue." He kept on talking to fill the silence. He would have Miss Welch do the proofreading. He mustn't risk such a pitiful fiasco again.

Sue made no answer.

He came back up from the basement with a plate of apples. He whistled all the way. He sat by her and pared the apple so carefully the peeling fell in one long red curl.

"I don't know whether Stephen'll think this paper

is as complete as it could be . . ." he went on talking.

He cut the apple into thin slivers and passed her one on the blade of the knife.

"It's so good, Dan."

"Northern Spy; there's nothing better." But when he took a bite himself, pity spoiled the flavor.

"When my hands are better, Dan, I'll do a better job. How soon will they be better?"

He said as he had said before, "It all takes time, Sue; you were pretty sick, you know." He leaned over and kissed her.

7

SUE knew when Dan came into the room that he was pleased about something. He let himself down into the arm chair and sat with his elbows on the arms, his hands half hiding his face.

"They asked me to give the Henry Fairchild lecture, Sue."

"And you'll be given the medal?"

Dan nodded. "Well, that's the natural inference." He was even more pleased now telling her about it than he had been before. "I was surprised."

Sue smiled. "I wish I could hear you give it."

"I wish so, too. Well, we'll see." But he was seeing himself give it. It would stir his corner of the medical world. He must have one of the boys run the slides; Kaplan could do that. And he'd have Whitney go over all the most recent literature again, although he had found nothing about it in his own careful search.

"We didn't think once, Sue, that this day would come, did we?"

"Of course we did." Sue's voice lagged behind her thoughts. She was going to say, "But not that I'd be like this when the time came," but she closed her lips on the words.

But when the day of the speech came Dan shook his head at the idea of her going.

"I don't think it would be wise, dear. I'll deliver the speech at a private hearing tomorrow and Jean can give you a full account of the rest of it."

Dan seemed abstracted, as though he did not notice her disappointment. There was a banquet first and she couldn't go to that, of course, but surely Dan could have managed her going to the lecture. She laid the blanket in pleats under her fingers so she would not look at Dan. The blanket was too wiry and kept escaping the pleats. She gave it up and smoothed it out again. Couldn't Dan feel that she was hurt?

But Dan stood by the window thinking about his paper. He didn't seem elated. He seemed almost troubled.

That evening he came in with Jean before they left.

"I wish you could go, Sue," Jean said. Jean was beautiful tonight.

"You aren't missing anything, dear," Dan told her.

"The thing didn't pan out the way I expected it to."

Dan was just saying that. Sue looked at them both enviously. She was so tired of being sick, of staying home!

As soon as the door closed behind them a frantic eagerness to be there possessed her. She had to be there. This meant recognition for Dan in the world beyond the little world of Woodstock.

When Agnes came up after her dinner she found Sue half standing, half leaning against the bed. She was trying to shake off her bed jacket that kept catching on her elbow.

"Mrs. Norton . . ." Agnes began calmly, hiding her surprise.

"Agnes, I'm going to hear Dr. Norton give the lecture, tonight. Will you help me dress?"

Agnes frowned ever so slightly. "Did Dr. Norton think you . . ." she broke off at her own stupidity. Anyone could see that Mrs. Norton was doing this on her own. She was so set on it, her color was high and her face had lost some of that slack look.

"I want that black chiffon," her tongue tripped over the word, "I used to have. I don't know where it is, you'll have to hunt it. Please hurry, it's so late."

Outside Mrs. Norton's room Agnes hesitated. She could take so long to find it it would be too late to go, but that was too mean. Or she could telephone the Academy and have Jean Keller called. But then Mrs.

Norton was so weak, she would give up the idea before she was ready to leave. If she just didn't have one of her crying spells when she had to give up.

Agnes found the black dress hung away in a case in the big closet off of Dr. Norton's room. It might do Mrs. Norton good just to get into a regular dress again.

Mrs. Norton was sitting on the couch. Her face looked tired when Agnes came in, or was it just that look? Her eyes were bright. She laughed.

"I wish you could have seen me pulling on the stocking. Half the time I'd miss it."

"You should have waited for me." Agnes had never heard her laugh before at her clumsiness.

It was hard getting on the dress. Mrs. Norton had the dead weight of the paralyzed. Agnes felt as though she were humoring a sick child. Some note of that crept into her voice.

"There, now let's see how you look!"

Mrs. Norton's silence made the remark sound foolish. But Mrs. Norton did look more like herself. The neck of the black dress with its facing of white gave her a self-sufficient air. The long close-fitting sleeves covered the woodenness of her arms.

"These slippers will do," Mrs. Norton said. She showed no sign of giving up. What would Dr. Norton think? Perhaps it was taking a chance to let her exert herself like this and get all excited. Mrs. Norton was holding herself quiet, as though to save her strength.

She was not distracted by the business of dressing. She didn't seem to hear Agnes.

"If you'll call a taxi, the driver can carry me down."

"Oh, Mrs. Norton, it's late now and . . ."

"I'll need my long coat. Jean may have put it away."

Agnes hunted the coat. All the time she worried about Dr. Norton. He would think she had no judgment. She stood on the stair holding the coat. If Tom were giving the Henry Fairchild lecture she would be there; oh, Lord, would she? If she had to be carried on a stretcher, she'd have to see Tom! Perhaps Mrs. Norton felt that way. Perhaps Dr. Norton didn't understand how she felt. She wouldn't live so very long. Agnes was nearly through with nursing. She was no longer the slave of what Miss Parsons, the superintendant of nurses, had taught her. She hurried upstairs with the coat.

Mrs. Norton was lying back but her eyes watched the door.

"Mrs. Norton, I know Dr. Norton will censure me for doing this." She had dropped back into Miss Parsons' phraseology.

"He knows I'm head-strong, Agnes; he won't blame you; please."

Mrs. Norton's pleading made her so pathetic, the poor darling.

Agnes called the taxi. "It's for an invalid. Could you send someone strong and gentle?" The taxi driver carried Mrs. Norton downstairs in his arms.

"The air smells good," Mrs. Norton said.

"You're not too cold?" Agnes asked in a worried voice.

Tonight she hardly felt the weather. The taxi smelled faintly of gasoline. Even that was pleasant to her. Agnes tucked pillows around her.

"Hurry," Sue said.

"Yes, hurry," Agnes urged.

University Avenue was a narrow passage-way between the walls of the cars parked along the curb. There was a special traffic policeman in front of Academy Hall. It all looked just as it had when it was hers, when she went in and out without thinking about it.

The taxi drove up to the entrance with a fine flourish. Sue could feel the flourish in her mind as well as in her body. The drive was like Dan's career, coming up with the Fairchild speech tonight as the final flourish. No, not final, he would go on becoming better known, and more distinguished.

"I think there's a wheel chair in the vestibule; I'll see," Agnes said.

Sue sat waiting. Now that she was here, it seemed so simple. Why hadn't Dan insisted on her coming? If he had only brought her, carrying her, himself! But he was so absorbed in his speech, the other part of her mind interposed quickly. He had worked for over three years on it; the speech tonight was the consummation of those three years' work.

"Not where I'll be conspicuous, under the gallery at

the back," Sue whispered jerkily. It mattered not at all that she was coming to the lecture in a chair, like an elderly woman. This was a triumphant night, hers as well as Dan's.

Even before the student usher pushed open the heavy door for them she heard Dan's voice. He was still nervous. There was that careful articulation and his voice was deeper than it was when he was at ease. He must be near the beginning. How well he looked! Under the lights he seemed a little pale. He still forgot about keeping his hands out of his pockets. After a while he would show slides to illustrate the lecture and she wouldn't be able to see him. It was good to see him in his own world again. It had been so long, he seemed a little strange. The strangeness crept like a cold draught into her happiness.

When Dan grew more technical she looked around. The same people here, in the same places, as though nothing had altered in this last year. She might never have been away. There were the Hutchins and Mary Boyer and Stephen and Stella Ridley.

Dan cared more about Stephen's judgment than anyone else's. Stephen would be proud of him. Perhaps they would drop in after the paper. Then she remembered; she had forgotten that the old friends didn't drop in anymore.

Jean was sitting next to Stella Ridley. Sue could only see the back of her head and the collar of her wrap. Sue watched Jean for some time. Jean's head was held so still, as though she were listening to every word Dan said. That was where she would have been sitting.

Sue wished Dan knew she was here. She would leave before the lights came on, before the lobby was crowded.

"If you will follow the slides you will see a graphic application of the principles I have been discussing."

The lights switched off. Charts were thrown on the screen. "A. B. female, age 37" was printed across the top of the chart. Dan paid no attention to the top line. His pointer was farther down the chart. But female, age 37, what of her? If a chart were made of her case it would read S. N. female, age 42. Charts were terrible things, hiding so much under figures and curves and initials.

The charts showed clearly on the screen. They were not much like the charts she had used to print for him, laboriously, for his first papers, with the lines a little crooked, sometimes.

Dan was through with the charts now. The lights came on above the stage. She must go quickly before he took his seat. She could linger in the back to see the medal presented. Dan was hesitating. He plunged both hands into the pockets of his coat. She wished she could see his face more clearly. She could tell so much from his mouth.

"This concludes my report of the work I have carried on for the last three years." Dan hesitated again. His voice altered. He seemed almost embarrassed.

"Yesterday, one of my instructors whom I had asked to look up any reference in the literature in the last four months came to me with a brief report in a Scandinavian medical journal of the work done by a young man in Bergen. By a strange coincidence, his approach to the problem, although from a different angle entirely, brought him to the same conclusions. His statistics show a greater number of cases over a period of nearly five years. His results check with mine, mine with his. I shall write him of my work. I take the keenest scientific pleasure in this added proof of my hypothesis, but, naturally, I cannot in honesty claim the priority for which you have honored me tonight."

For a few seconds she had been more taken up with the sight of Dan than with what he was saying. He was very nervous. He was still speaking with an effort. "Naturally I cannot in honesty claim the priority . . ." Dan had said.

When Dan started working on this, she could remember so clearly, it was during the mid-semester lull, he told her there wasn't a soul who had published a thing on it. If he could prove his theory he would have something . . . she raised one shaking hand to her mouth. She did not know that she bit her knuckles.

He had counted on this. "My contribution to real progress," he had said. Dan had spent his two months' vacation working with white rats that summer in Baltimore although he had planned to go north to the lake. But she had not minded. It was as though a secret excitement was with them so that even the hot air of Baltimore had freshness and stir. And he had worked so hard on it ever since. Now there was no point in all that time spent. He wasn't the first, after all. The medal was given for an original contribution.

Why hadn't he told her as soon as he knew? That was why he hadn't taken her.

"It was too late last evening to cancel the occasion tonight. At any rate, I have been happy to have the opportunity of talking about a procedure which I believe constitutes a tremendous advance. But the individuals who push ahead our knowledge inch by inch are unimportant, even the great ones. It is the knowledge itself that is important. I thank you."

Dan, oh, Dan! She wished all the people were away. He was wonderful standing there. He needn't have told about the man off in Bergen. No one here would have known. Then she was ashamed of her own thought.

The auditorium was more still than if it had been empty. Dan's figure blurred for Sue as he walked across the platform and took his seat. Sue knocked the tears out of her eyes. She glanced up for Agnes. Agnes had stepped away from the wheel chair so she could see. Sue moved her hand awkwardly to beckon her.

The terrible heavy silence snapped into fragments of noise, someone began clapping in the balcony, someone on the platform, then everyone was clapping. Stephen Ridley rose. Stella and Jean and Hutchins rose; everyone was standing. Everyone was standing but Dan down there on the platform and herself here in the obscure corner in the wheel chair.

"Look, they're going to give him the medal anyway; I should think they would!" Agnes murmured.

The president was walking toward the lectern. It was more than she could stand. The stupid tears ran out of her eyes, tears of pride, tears of anger.

"We'd better go," she whispered.

Agnes nodded, but she made no move to go.

"This medal has never been bestowed on any more distinguished gentleman than Dr. Daniel Norton . . ." Instant applause drowned his words. There was the sound of a cheer up in the gallery, a cheer in a young voice.

Dan sat so quietly up there. He was touched but he didn't like this sort of thing. Their medal was too like giving a reward to a good boy for effort rather than accomplishment. Dan must feel let down. They didn't understand. She understood. She was ready to go now. She must be home when Dan came.

Agnes propelled the chair slowly out through the door into the lobby. It had a squeak it had not had before. The lobby was cold after the packed room. It was all so familiar. The plaster bust of Caesar, the drinking fountain, the telephone booth in the corner to the right.

"I'll call the taxi," Agnes said.

Sue sat in the lobby trying to catch sounds from behind the closed doors. They were clapping as though they would never stop. The student ushers pushed open the doors and fastened them back. She could not see the platform from here.

"Agnes, never mind about the taxi. I've decided to wait for Dr. Norton. I must see him." Her words trickled out like water from a leaking faucet, two or three together, then one.

Agnes was worried. Dr. Norton might not approve. The crowds might be harmful to Mrs. Norton.

"Hadn't you better go before the crowds?" she urged tentatively. Sue shook her head.

The people were coming out now. Agnes drew the wheel chair over to one side in the jut made by the telephone booth. Tonight Sue didn't mind being seen. She was elated, lifted above her body by pride in Dan, above Mrs. Rathman's pity and the curiosity shining out of Mrs. Ayers' small blue eyes. They had heard she talked with difficulty and they were afraid to come over and speak to her. But tonight Sue looked at them with cool detachment.

"There's Mrs. Keller," Agnes said. "I'll tell her you are here."

"No . . . I . . . I'll wait till Dr. Norton comes."

She saw Dan before Agnes did. He was coming out with Dr. Robbins. He was only half listening.

"There he is, Agnes."

Agnes touched his arm. He turned quickly. His eyes brightened. "You took matters into your own hands and came, Sue! I was going to spare you this. It turned out to be a regular old melodrama. I didn't mean it to."

"I know." She understood him so well; she loved him so much.

Dan wheeled the chair along the hall. Everyone wanted to talk to Dan. Stephen Ridley came up. In his dry, unemotional voice he said, "We're proud of him, Sue. He's an ornament to the profession."

Blessed Stephen! He didn't even look surprised to see her there. He acted as though she were always there.

"Dan has taught his young men more tonight than he could have in years of teaching, Sue."

Jean hurried over to them. "Sue, how fine! I'm so glad you came. Dan didn't want you to know, he thought you'd be so disappointed." Jean ran her sentences together in her excitement.

They were a little group in the middle of the hall. The people thronging out looked at them curiously; at Dan, at his invalid wife, at Jean. Sue saw the picture they made. This was new to her, this standing aside and seeing herself and others.

"Jean, you and Dan are coming up to the house . . . why, Sue! I didn't know you were here; it's wonderful to see you." Alice Hutchins kissed her.

Sue had never noticed before how Alice flushed when she was embarrassed. Alice was embarrassed now at coming so suddenly on her.

"It will be like old times, Sue. I've been wanting to come to see you, but Hutch kept saying I'd tire you; that you'd soon be well and to wait till then." Poor Alice, she was such an affectionate person. She was worried lest she had hurt her feelings asking Dan and Jean.

Sue smiled but was silent. If she spoke Alice would be shocked at the sound of her words. Instead she glanced at Dan.

"Thank you, Alice, not tonight," Dan said.

"Sue, I just heard you were here." Stella Ridley was good to see again, her homely, distinguished face, her too sharp eyes and wide mouth. Stella had been her closest friend. But even Stella had stayed away these last months.

"Well, the sacrifice of the individual to the scientific ideal is a great thing, isn't it?" Stella commented. "A halo is rather becoming to Dan." Stella's face reflected the sarcasm of her words for an instant, then softened into affectionate humor.

"Perforce, Stella," Dan defended himself. "At the time, I thought it was the only thing to do. Now it seems like mock heroics."

"Oh, no, Dan." Stella raised her eyebrows in comic protest.

Every aspect of this evening stood out for Sue. Nothing was blurred. The succession of images was so vivid it began to tire her. People, old acquaintances, acted almost afraid of her. They looked at her and then were careful to look away. Their surprise at seeing her here where she used always to be was so clear it made her feel like someone else, someone strange.

Dan pushed the chair on down the hall to the door. The corridor had never been so long before.

Jean murmured that she would go on with MacLean unless Sue wanted her to stay.

The Keiths and the Whitneys came up to them. Dan paused again. Sue smiled at them.

"I felt I should have burned that Norwegian reference, Dan," Peter said. Dan laughed. He seemed to enjoy these younger men more than his old friends.

"You must feel very proud," Prudence Keith said. She looked at her, Sue felt, without shyness, but Prudence had not know her any other way.

"Yes, I am," Sue managed.

"Dr. Norton was wonderful!" Elsa said.

Sue had almost forgotten Agnes standing near her chair. "Agnes, Dr. Norton will get me home, you go on with your husband."

Then she and Dan were finally alone in the car. She was tired—*so tired*. But Dan mustn't know that.

Dan reached out for her hand. "You had to come, dear!"

"Of course."

"It was a little flat."

"No, you were fine, Dan."

He shook his head. "Just honest. I shouldn't care as

long as the principle is getting across, but I do, Sue."

Sue smiled in the dark.

"I know," she said.

8

THE morning after the lecture, Sue woke late. Her head ached. Her legs, stretched out under the covers, had no connection with the rest of her body. She turned and her whole body was stiff. She closed her eyes again, not wanting to see anybody. She knew it was late because the house was so quiet. She heard Agnes arrange her tray on the bedside table.

"The coffee first," Sue said. Her words seemed to slur more than usual. Agnes couldn't understand her. She tried again. It was because her mouth was dry. After the coffee she would be able to talk more clearly.

Agnes held the coffee cup, tilting the glass straw toward her. Coffee through the straw wasn't like coffee drunk from a cup. She pushed the straw away and felt the edge of the cup against her lip. She let her teeth come against the china. The coffee in her throat was full-flavored and hot. It made her feel better.

"I can hold it now."

She held the cup in both hands, bending her head to the cup so she wouldn't have to move her hands. It would be so good to pour Dan's coffee again.

"Is the cup too hot?" Agnes asked, hovering over her.

"No," Sue said.

She could manage very well. The heat of the liquid coming through the china warmed her finger-tips. The smooth, bowl-shaped cup was comforting. Only the handle was stem-like and hard to hold. Her fingers couldn't feel it easily.

Agnes turned swiftly as Sue caught her breath. The handle had escaped her fingers. The half cup of coffee had spilled on the lace at her breast, soaking through on her skin and splashed an ugly stain on the light blue of her bed jacket.

"It didn't burn, did it?" Agnes asked anxiously. Sue shook her head with a little moan. She closed her eyes.

Then Jean came in to bring the morning paper, before Agnes could lift a warning finger.

"Oh, you poor dear, Sue! Isn't drinking coffee in bed the hardest thing!" Her voice was sympathetic, even off-handed. But Sue could feel it taking pains to be. She wouldn't open her eyes to look at Jean.

"I feel a little dizzy," she murmured faintly, pretending. Better that than to be clumsy. She closed her eyes while Agnes and Jean helped her take off the soaked gown and jacket.

"You wouldn't think a cup of coffee could do so much damage," Agnes said, as though it were the coffee's fault, as though she were a child.

"I'll have my bath now. I don't want any more," Sue murmured. But what had happened? How had she done it? Her hands were no steadier. She felt tired, so tired and discouraged. The day was spoiled.

"Were you ever so thrilled as at Dan last night, Sue?" Jean asked. "And this morning, he didn't even want to talk about it."

Sue had forgotten the night before. Now it all came back to her. She had felt so well last night, driving down in the taxi. Her mind went back over every detail: the moment when someone in the gallery had cheered Dan. But even that cheer had been hollow to Dan; he was disappointed.

Sue felt Stella's eyes on her again, so sharp, so kind. Alice Hutchins with the flush mounting in her face, embarrassed at seeing her.

She felt hot again under the eyes of those strangers who used to be her friends. She didn't want to see them again until she could speak clearly. The stiffness didn't matter so much as the speech did.

But was she any better? Why didn't her speech clear more quickly. Dan said it was a temporary thing. . . .

"Are you very tired after the lecture, Sue? It was lovely to see you there and I know Dan loved it." Jean perched on the window-seat.

"No, not very," Sue said.

"Before I knew you were going to the lecture, I arranged for the barber to come this afternoon. You know we talked about how much better your hair would look; and it will be so much easier to take care of. But if you don't feel like having it done today, we can postpone it."

Suddenly Sue dreaded any stranger coming. "I don't think I want it cut," she said.

"Oh, Sue, we went all over that. It will be lots better, won't it, Agnes?"

"I think it would be becoming, and it would be much easier," Agnes said gently. "Your hair is lovely and soft, Mrs. Norton."

Sue reached up and felt the big braid of hair that was wound around her head. "Dan likes it long," she said.

"He just thinks he does. When he sees it short he'll like it that way," Jean said.

"All right," Sue said. She didn't care. Perhaps her head wouldn't ache so if her hair were short.

The barber was a matter-of-fact person, small, colorless, a tired look above his sandy mustache. He was new in Woodstock. Jean said all the college girls went to him. He spoke with a foreign accent.

"It would be much better cut," he assured her. "You have too much, and when you lie down, even against a pillow, it gets mussed." His hands suggested the impossibility of long hair.

"But my hair is straight," Sue persisted.

"It isn't exactly straight. It curls around your face, don't you know it does? And hair as dark as yours, Sue, is very striking short."

The barber moved the bed so the sunlight fell clearly on her face.

"I want to see," Sue said.

Agnes turned the dresser so she could see herself in the mirror. Sue looked at herself, propped up against the pillows. How pale she looked. Something was different about her eyes. Her mouth was queer.

"Do the scissors feel cold?" the barber asked.

She smiled at him. Then she glanced in the mirror again. Her smile seemed unnatural. The left corner of her mouth had no part in the smile. She tried smiling again. Agnes was watching her. She saw that Agnes looked away.

"It's going to be lovely, Sue," Jean said.

"It's very becoming, Mrs. Norton," Agnes said.

But Sue only glanced at her hair. It was well enough. It did wave back from her face. But she didn't care any more about her hair. It was her face; was it changed? When the barber was gone she would ask Agnes.

"You could keep the hair and have it made into a fine braid," the barber said, holding it up in his hand.

She looked at it as he brushed it across his wrist, but it was no longer her hair. Hair should be alive, like flame, free to the wind. It was dead, cut off, held up in the barber's hand. She remembered the feeling of her doll's wig. It would be like that.

"Do you feel like Samson, Sue?" Jean asked lightly.

"Yes," Sue said without smiling. The barber and

Agnes laughed. But the laughs had no body. "I don't want it any more," Sue said. The hair was repugnant to her.

Jean went downstairs with the barber. Now was the time to ask Agnes about her face. Agnes was pushing the dresser back so she couldn't see in the mirror.

"Don't move it. I look . . ." Sue began. But if her face were changed Agnes wouldn't tell her. Agnes always said she was better. Perhaps Agnes only said that. But Dan always told her the truth. Dan was the one to ask.

"Are you getting up or would you rather rest after last night?"

Of course she was getting up. She was up every day now. She was through staying in bed. Tonight Dan would take her downstairs. But her body lay heavily against the bed. She was tired today.

"I'll stay in bed until evening," Sue said. Dan wouldn't be home until evening. She would save her strength until then. She wouldn't ask Agnes anything. Maybe Agnes tried to keep the dresser turned that way so she couldn't see how thick her face looked.

She pulled the cover up around her and closed her eyes against the warm light of the room. She felt like hiding away from the people at the lecture, from Jean, from Agnes. Her heart was pounding foolishly, the way it used to when she was a little girl, running a race with Jean. She could always run away from Jean when they raced. It was as though she were running away from something now. She took a long breath to stop the foolish trembling.

That afternoon Jean went from Mrs. Stevens' luncheon down to buy a new negligee for Sue.

As usual, at the luncheon, everyone had asked how Sue was. Alice Hutchins had said, "It must be such a comfort to Sue to have you there." But she wondered if she were any comfort to Sue. She wanted to be. This morning when Sue spilled her cup of coffee she had felt so sorry for her and yet she had felt that Sue wished she weren't there. All the time she was helping Agnes change the bed she had felt it couldn't really be, that this person wasn't Sue, her older sister who had used to have the other bed in her room when they were children.

Sitting in the small, discreet fitting room waiting for the saleswoman to bring the negligees, Jean tried to remember Sue as she used to be. At sixteen, Sue had had a coral-colored party dress and worn her hair pinned up in curls in back. Jean had knelt in her nightgown behind the spindles of the stairs and watched the boy who took Sue to the dance hold her coat and laugh about something. He had looked at Sue as though he thought her beautiful, too. Jean had gone back upstairs to bed and hugged her knees up under her chin in delight. She had meant to be just like Sue when she was sixteen.

Jean remembered her mother saying, "Sue never

had tantrums, Jean!" And she had covered her head with a pillow and kicked at the foot-board until someone came and closed the door. She had hated Sue then. But afterwards Sue came in secretly and brought her a piece of cake from dinner.

"Don't be mad at nothing, Jeanie," Sue had said.

The saleswoman came back in. "Of course, right now, our stock is a little limited. At the beginning of the season we get in just the tailored things for the co-eds."

Sue had been a co-ed. She had met Dan here. Sue had come home one vacation and told Jean about Dan. She had hidden his pin in her handkerchief box and only Jean knew about it.

"This is almost a hostess gown," the saleswoman went on. You could wear it for little informal dinners at home. Would you like to try it on?"

"It's for my sister, but we're about the same size," Jean said. Green had always been one of her own favorite colors. Sue had always worn coral and blue and gray.

"Pardon me, but you're Mrs. Norton's sister, aren't you? I used to wait on Mrs. Norton and there is a resemblance. How is she?" The sympathy in the woman's voice irked Jean. Everyone in this town knew all about everyone else. The faculty and their lives were common property.

"I always used to wait on her when she came in here. The last time she was in, she bought a beige chiffon for a reception she was going to; we had to take it in, I remember."

Sue never should wear beige, Jean thought. Sue never did buy the right things.

"Is she getting better?"

Jean looked at the genuine concern in the saleswoman's face. "The improvement is very slow, of course," Jean answered automatically, as she had at the luncheon today. "We really can't tell yet." That was it, there was nothing decisive. They were all living in an atmosphere of waiting.

Jean slipped on the green robe, girding it tightly at the waist. Sue was about her height. Jean moved one arm so the sleeve swung gracefully. She looked at herself in the mirror, seeing Sue whose face was deadened of all quick expression; remembering how all Sue's flesh when she helped her on with the fresh gown was so rigid her own hands avoided the touch. It was hateful to see at the same time how straight and slim she herself was.

"It's very becoming to you," the saleswoman said, but Jean felt as though her own thought had drawn it from her. She turned away from the mirror and slipped off the negligee. What kind of a person was she that she could admire herself and shrink from Sue because she was ill? How could Sue endure the sight of herself changing? Or didn't she see the change? How could she take pleasure in pretty gowns and negligees? It was so pitiful.

"Wrap it up, please," she said. "I'll take it with me." The fact that it was much more than she had thought of paying comforted her. She had bought it for herself, after all, as much as for Sue. It was hard to see Sue so changed. This morning Sue had seemed very little interested even in talking about Dan's paper. She had read the flattering newspaper accounts without a comment. Perhaps when people were so sick they became more and more wrapped up in themselves.

Instead of going back to the car and hurrying home, Jean turned in at the Engineers' Arch and followed the trail of students across the diagonal. The college buildings made a sheltered square. Even with the murmur of voices and the constant exchange of greetings there was a quietness in here. Jean had only been here once before. The grassy squares between the walks were littered with thin brown leaves, but the ivy leaves that still clung to the walls of the buildings were as glossy as polished leather. But even here the late November day was depressing, lonely. Each person was so alone: Sue in her sickness, she, herself, unable to help Sue. Sometimes she felt she hardly knew Donna. And Dan must be lonely, too.

Dan would be through at the hospital in another hour. She could stop at a drugstore and call him; tell him she would be waiting out in front when he was ready. She had never done that before. He wouldn't mind. He might be glad to get away.

"Yes?" Dan's voice was brisk over the phone.

"Dan, I was downtown. I thought I'd call and see if there was a chance of your leaving a little early."

"I'll be through in a few minutes; come right on over," Dan said.

Had he seemed glad to hear her? An unreasoning eagerness filled her.

9

DAN was glad to reach the hospital these mornings. He came over earlier and he was slower to leave in the evenings, unless Jean came by to drive him home. He spent more time sitting in his office looking out the window at the valley. He could see a long way now that the trees were bare. The hills and the fields had turned to brown without his knowing it and yet he had looked out this window every day. The change was as complete and imperceptible in its coming as the change in Sue, he thought, staring at the slow curve of the bank. The river had a thin scum of ice over it this morning.

He and Sue had used to skate on the river where it widened out below the bridge. But he hadn't been down there in a long time. If Jean came over for him this evening they might drive home over the river road.

"Time for your ward round, Dr. Norton," Miss Welch stopped in to say.

"Yes, I was just going."

Miss Welch had been his secretary for a long time. She looked at him now with compassion in her eyes. He felt the compassion and shrugged it off uncomfortably, stepping a little more briskly as he went down the hall.

When he stepped off the elevator on the fourth floor the group was already waiting. All the sun of the corridor seemed concentrated on the fresh white coats and uniforms. Dan smiled; Stanton Keith in his long white instructor's coat looked as though the weight of the hospital rested on his shoulders. The two interns in their short white coats and trousers had the usual arrogantly superior attitude toward the group of senior medical students.

Sue used to call it the "arrogance of the white coat," he remembered. She even insisted that she could tell the ratings of the professors and assistant professors by the air with which they wore their coats. Perhaps she was right; Ridley wore his white coat as though it were an old laboratory smock, Hutchins his as though it were a Prince Albert. He must remember to tell Sue that.

A nurse bustled out to join the group. Even the nurses looked more stiffly starched on days of ward rounds.

"Good morning," he said to the whole group.

"Norton's in a good mood, I wouldn't mind giving the history this morning," the senior medical student named Stevens murmured to the man next to him.

"When I give a history the old boy's usually on the prod!"

They moved down the ward together, Dan and Keith ahead. "Well, Keith, what have you this morning?"

"Two new cases came in yesterday, sir, one's a good one."

"Let's see that one first."

Dan glanced around the ward with satisfaction. The ward round made him think of a barracks inspection. The patients always responded. Later in the day when their temperatures were up and the beds became uncomfortable they had more complaints, but now, at the beginning of the morning, fresh from their baths, they tried to feel their best. The progress of the group from bed to bed carried an air of hope with it. They came to the bed farthest over.

"This is Mrs. Stringer, Dr. Norton; she felt pretty badly when she came in yesterday, but she feels more rested this morning," Keith said.

"How do you do." Dan shook hands with Mrs. Stringer. He smiled at her reassuringly at the same time that he noticed her yellowish color, the thinness of her arms, the enlargement of the abdomen.

"Let's have the story," Dan said, thinking how much better Keith handled the patient, how much more assured he seemed than he had in the beginning. Keith had been eager to have him see the patient. Endicott, one of the students, was giving the history. Dan saw

Keith frown at his inept marshaling of facts. They all had to learn, though.

Mrs. Stringer's listlessness had changed to alert interest in her own case. Dan nodded at her as her eyes sought his trying to read what he thought. He noticed Ward, the junior intern studying Mrs. Stringer with an expression of genuine concern on his round young face.

Dan interrupted the list of negative findings. "What do you think the possibilities are, Endicott?"

The student hesitated, flushing. "Well, I don't know what to think . . ." he began. Dan could see Keith's impatience at having his best case so poorly presented.

"Well, Dr. Keith?"

"Why, from the history alone, it's cancer of the . . ." He said it promptly, clearly. The word fell into complete silence. The group around the bed seemed almost to sway as by a breath. Dan glanced quickly back to Mrs. Stringer. Her gaunt face was twisted in fright. Her mouth trembled. She was staring at him pitifully. Dan took her hand in his. He made his voice very casual.

"Mrs. Stringer, Dr. Keith means to say that that is one of the possibilities. He realizes that you're quite ill and that's one of the possibilities we must rule out. We're so glad you came in as soon as you did. Go on, Keith." He mustn't make too much of this.

But Mrs. Stringer was staring at Keith. Why didn't Keith go on? In all his years of ward rounds he'd never had even a student blurt out like that before a patient; there were so many ways of saying things. Keith's face had lost all of its color. He looked sick enough to faint. Dan saw young Ward move away and stare out the window. He saw the little curly-headed nurse look indignantly at Keith. Mrs. Stringer was sobbing now.

"Now, Mrs. Stringer, you're a sensible woman, you can understand that we discuss the gravest possibilities in all these cases but that doesn't mean . . ." his voice went on. Mrs. Stringer gave a gallant hiccough in her effort to stop crying, but her disbelief stood in her eyes. "I'll be back to see you after the ward round, then we'll go over the situation," he told her.

"Suppose we take the other new case first, Keith." He wondered if Keith was going to be sick on the spot. He had lost all his assurance. He turned the pages of his note-book back and forth as though he couldn't read what he saw there. The little nurse was glaring at him.

"I . . . Dr. MacLean can give you the case, sir."

"All right, let's have it, MacLean." Dan made his voice cheerful.

Keith was walking out. Dan kept his eyes on the new patient, but he heard Keith's footsteps going the length of the ward. He heard the door at the end swing closed. He felt the group move uncomfortably.

"Well, we'll see what this diet we're going to put you on will do," he told the fat old lady. "But we don't want your husband smuggling in any sauerkraut and frankfurters or even a cruller to you!" The old lady chuckled but none of the group around the bed even smiled. He could feel their tenseness as though they were holding themselves in ready to burst with indignation the second they were off the ward.

He cut the round short and went back alone to see Mrs. Stringer. He remembered Sue once asking him if the patients didn't mind being discussed before the students.

"Why, no, I don't think so; it's all in the way it's done, of course. They know we're as interested in helping them to get well as they are," he had told her. But you didn't expect a thing like this. Keith was as sensitive as any one of the group. He wondered just what he could say to Mrs. Stringer. He drew up a chair beside her bed.

"Doctor, I was just thinking; my grandmother died of cancer, but she had a bad fall. . . ."

Dan drew a breath of relief; she could face the word, anyway. He listened sympathetically to all the long garrulous reminiscences. It was better to let her talk first.

When he went back to his office he half expected to find Keith there, but Miss Welch said he hadn't been in. He had her call his home to see if Keith had gone there. He was sorry he hadn't seen him before he left.

Once, during the afternoon, Dan dropped into the staff-room in time to hear one of the interns saying, "If Keith were a junior medical student, but an instructor shouting out cancer like that in front of a patient! It was dinged into us when we were freshmen . . ."

"We all of us do queer things at times," Dan snapped out sharply at the boy.

But Dan thought about Keith all day: Endicott's stupid inability to arrange his findings had tried him; it had been a case he had worked up and he was sure of his diagnosis. Keith was so often harassed by doubts about his diagnosis . . . that must have been it. He had spoken without thinking, of course.

About four in the afternoon Dan was standing at the window in his office looking down the valley. It was bleak enough now that the sky had turned cloudy. The river no longer glittered, but was only a dark line marking the edge of the bank. Then he saw a single figure walking across the cornfield. The wind blew across the bare ground and billowed his coat around him so that he looked like a moving scarecrow.

Dan studied the scarecrow. It was Keith. He watched him kick at something on the ground; a rotten pumpkin split into bright yellow fragments and rolled off against a corn-shock. The act was eloquent of Keith's whole sick disgust. Dan watched him climb the rise of ground beyond the cornfield, a lonely figure against the bare country. He disappeared around the clump of trees. He must have gone straight from the ward down along the river, crossed at the bridge and struck out on the other side for the open country.

He must see Keith the first thing in the morning. He was taking it too hard. If he weren't worth worrying about he wouldn't take it so hard.

"Who was it, Agnes?" Sue asked that evening when Agnes came back from answering the door.

"It's Stanton Keith. He wants to see Dr. Norton. He's going to wait. I told him his wife had phoned to see if he were here, just after dinner. He's calling her now."

"Let him come up and wait here," Sue said. Sometimes she did as she would have done before she was sick. It was only when she had time to think that she shrank from human contacts.

Stanton Keith hesitated on the threshold of the room. He had only seen Mrs. Norton a few times, and then briefly. He was disheveled from walking so long in the wind. His shoes were gray with dust. He was hungry and tired and worried. He could have no rest until he had seen Dan. He was impatient now at having to talk to Mrs. Norton.

"How do you do, Mrs. Norton?"

"Good evening." She was learning to sit completely still when people were with her, her tremor disturbed them so. She was glad that Stanton Keith had come in. Jean had gone to a play with young MacLean and Dan was over at Stephen Ridley's.

Keith sat down on the stool by the fire.

"I wanted to see Dr. Norton. I . . . I did a cruelly

stupid thing today on the ward round." His face flushed as he spoke. The terrific need in him to talk to someone broke down his natural reserve. He hardly knew Mrs. Norton, but the quiet room brought it out of him. "I said, right in front of a woman on the ward, that . . . that she had cancer. Dan, Dr. Norton, passed it off, but he could have murdered me right there. I don't blame him. I got out and I haven't been back since. He must think me a fool." Keith looked at Sue.

Her face showed neither sympathy nor disgust. Sympathy would have embarrassed him; disgust would have stopped him. She was slow in speaking. The queer, sing-song slurring of her voice made it impersonal.

"Dan wasn't really angry." She had to wait between her sentences so they wouldn't slur together. "I know he understood how it happened. If he seemed angry, that was for the example. I don't believe anyone is really cruel without . . . meaning to be." There was a long pause and then she said, "Knowing the truth . . . couldn't hurt . . . that woman the way hoping and wondering would."

Suddenly some fiber of her voice, or the unusual intensity of her eyes made Stanton Keith realize that what Sue was saying she was bringing up out of her own experience; it wasn't just a remark made to comfort him. It was a fact she was thinking out as she said it. What a thing to talk about with her! She must have doubts about her own condition. Sweat broke out on him. He stood up, badly confused.

"Thank you, Mrs. Norton, I . . ." He had meant to say something about being sorry, but the words miraculously disappeared under his tongue. "I'll see Dr. Norton tomorrow; I haven't been home yet . . . good night."

She let him go without a word, staring at him. He saw her raise one hand jerkily to her mouth. But her face had the same vacant look. He avoided her eyes.

Outside the house, he heard Dan coming along the drive. He waited. He had come up here just to see Dan, because he had to talk to him. Now he didn't want to see him. He tried to think what he should say. The whole scene this morning came back to him, the look of disgust on Dan's face. He reached the bottom of the porch steps just as Dan came up the side path.

"Hello, Keith, I've been wanting to see you." Dan's voice was cordial.

"Dr. Norton, I . . ." He stopped and looked off into the darkness of the shrubbery to find his words.

"Sit down a moment, won't you, Stan? It's early yet."

They sat down on the steps. Stanton found himself lighting a cigarette from Dan's match. He found himself looking into the warm, lighted hollow Dan's hands made around the flame. Beyond was the bleakness of the frozen road he had walked this afternoon.

"Dr. Norton, I don't know what kind of an ass you must think me." It was easier to talk looking straight ahead down the drive.

"Stan, you're taking this morning too hard. I was sorry you got away before I had a chance to see you. I've been concerned about you all day."

"The second I'd said it, Dan, I would have done anything to . . . I had to get out of there. I've been walking all afternoon and evening, trying to get the look of Mrs. Stringer's face out of my mind. Did she stop crying?"

"Oh, yes." Dan's voice was slow, natural. "Tomorrow morning I think you'll find she wants to talk to you about her case."

"I wanted to speak to you about that. I wondered if it wouldn't be better for me not to go back up there; if I could take my vacation now perhaps. I imagine the story has gone the rounds by now."

Dan threw his cigarette away before he spoke. The glowing end described an arc that ended with a wet sizzle on the damp ground. It was cold on the porch step. Dan buttoned up the neck of his overcoat. He glanced at Stan sitting there, nursing his hurt and humiliation. That was uppermost now, even more than his feeling for Mrs. Stringer. He understood. Personal vanity bulked large in the best of men, disguised under ambition, under sensitiveness, under driving-power.

"Keith, that's a slip that any one of us can understand. You'll never make a mistake like that again. It wasn't done out of indifference. As far as the hospital is concerned, tomorrow there will be something else to talk about."

"Dan, I . . ." For the life of him, he couldn't tell Dan that it was such a relief to be sure of a diagnosis that he had forgotten everything but that. Dan expected him to be sure.

"I understand; you were so carried away by the fact that Mrs. Stringer's case made a perfect text-book picture that you forgot everything else. If a layman heard you he'd think you an unfeeling brute. But if it weren't for the eagerness we can feel over some of these things, he couldn't hire us to take care of his whining colds and backaches for love or money."

Dan stood up. "Mrs. Norton's light is on. I want to see her before she goes to sleep. Don't worry any more. Tomorrow when you see Mrs. Stringer, don't make any apology, just take some extra time with her, let her talk to you about her fears. Be truthful with her and gentle, it will probably help her more than not knowing."

"Do you really think so?" Stan asked incredulously.

"Keith, the more patients I see, the more I doubt the wisdom of trying to keep people in the dark about the nature of their disease." His voice was lower, as though he were talking to himself. "It's a humane instinct, all right, but every intelligent person has doubts when she doesn't feel her condition improving any. I wonder if it isn't better to tell her and help her face it . . . well, you won't bedevil yourself any longer, will you?" He shook Keith's hand in a quick, strong grasp.

Stanton started down the drive. Then he stopped.

"Dan, I suppose I was pretty well worked up when I came over here to talk to you tonight." He scuffed the gravel under his foot. "Mrs. Norton knew I was waiting to see you and she asked me to come upstairs." He looked at Dan. Dan nodded. "Well, somehow, I found myself telling her about the whole thing. I hadn't talked to anybody since morning. I . . . I just wondered if it would have worried her?"

"Oh, no, Sue's heard plenty about illness in her day," Dan reassured him. "Don't worry about that." But he wondered as he walked softly to Sue's door.

At first she seemed asleep, she lay so still, not reading, but her eyes were open. She spoke at once.

"Dan?"

When he sat down by her she said slowly, "You saw . . ."

"Keith, yes." Dan took pains to speak lightly. "He said he had to tell you all about it. Funny thing; he's the last person I'd expect to blurt out a thing like that in front of a patient. He was pretty much upset."

"You were nice to him, Dan?"

"Oh, yes, he's a good man. The thing was just one of those terrible slips."

"What about the woman?" Sue asked.

"She was upset, of course, but she talked calmly when I left. I told her it was only a possibility, that we had to have x-rays, perhaps an exploratory operation to make sure." He watched Sue as he talked.

Sue's face showed no expression.

Could he go on from talking of the woman with cancer to find out whether Sue would rather know the truth about herself?

"And then what will you tell her?" Sue asked. She lifted her head from the pillow. Dan noticed how her neck had stiffened. She used to hold her head so bravely. And when she dropped her head back he had always wanted to kiss the white arch of her throat. He kissed the stiff column of her throat now.

"Dan, what will you tell her?"

"Oh, we'll be guided by circumstances. If she has a family, we'll tell them first." This would be an opportunity, but he shrank from worrying her.

"She must know pretty well after he said that."

Dan nodded. "I'm afraid so."

After a long pause Sue said, "You could see how the boy felt. He was all tired out."

She was thinking about Keith now instead of the woman. She hadn't gone from thinking of her to wondering about herself, Dan thought with relief.

"Good night, dear."

Sue lay still and let him bend down to kiss her. Her silence bothered him. He turned out her light and opened the window.

"It's starting to snow," he said.

She made no answer. He hesitated. Sometimes he felt like a stranger with Sue.

"Pretty good day, dear?"

"All the days are the same," she said slowly.

"Well, tomorrow evening we're having the youngsters all over here for a little supper. Either I'll take you downstairs or have them come up here for cocktails," he said briskly.

"I'm better off in bed," Sue said, almost sullenly.

But she was tired tonight,—this was just a mood, he told himself.

10

SUE watched the snow that fell steadily outside the window. It was lighter than the sky. Invisible if she looked straight up into the air, it emerged suddenly out of the atmosphere; bright, swift, soft. The snow blocked out the limitations of the back garden, the garage, and the winding driveway. She watched it, wishing it would snow harder and harder. Why did it seem as though it must be falling to the sound of music? She could almost hum the tune. If she were out in it she wouldn't think of the music; the soft, moist stillness would be enough.

She leaned her head back against the pillows and closed her eyes. Now she could feel the snow, falling on her face, getting in her eyes so that she had to blink. If she put her hand up to her head her hair would be slightly damp. The air would be cold . . . the wanting to be out in it deepened to an anguish that stung at her eyes. Instead of snow, there were tears on her face.

This was the only interval of the day when she was left alone, she reflected, unless she were sleeping. Jean had just gone down with the tea things. Agnes had gone out for a walk. Dan would be home soon.

Agnes had brushed her hair for her before she left and helped her into the new green negligee Jean had given her. She had moved over to the couch, but she wouldn't let Dan carry her downstairs. What was the use?

It was darker outside. The snow along the railing of the little balcony gleamed white. The branches of the beech trees were limned with it, even the little twigs. In the room the gas fire was red, cozy, synthetic; the room with its magazines and books and radio threw up an artificial sense of content. With difficulty she reached up and turned off the light over her head. Her hand shook so it hit against the shade and set it rattling.

The evening outside came closer. The snow fell swiftly, whitely into silence. She was alone, hurrying down University Avenue, her mind on errands; no time for watching the snow and heedless of its soft falling, passing people she knew, smiling, nodding, going on with her own pleasant way of life . . . but she had only to look away from the window to see how far removed she was from that old life.

When she was over this . . . she kept her eyes

steadily on the dark; the falling snow was scarcely visible so far from the window, each flake a tiny self figure in some dark silk. There was sheen on the silk from the lighted windows downstairs . . . she couldn't keep her mind busy any longer . . . she should have guessed from the beginning. Dan should have told her.

All day she had staved off thinking except when her thoughts pierced through her drowsiness like sudden pain. After last night she had been too tired to do anything but sleep.

She wondered with the timid curiosity of a woman who had never had a child if childbirth were not like this: the night of pain so intense she felt she couldn't bear it, then a little respite when she thought of other things, then the pain again, more agonizing than before. It was no less real because the agony was in her brain. On and on and on until the life within hers was taken away and she was left empty and exhausted. This was the way women must feel who found the life they had carried under their hearts had died; just as empty. All these months she had clung to the belief that she was getting better. But that belief was dead now.

She had had little doubts, but she had buried them underneath her faith in what Dan and Stephen and Agnes and Jean said. She had felt herself growing stronger, apart, that is, from her limbs and her face and her voice. But looking back she could see what a fool she had been.

Alone in the night she had gone back and forth over all the last few months; things Dan had said, the way he had looked. They had not been so insistent about rest lately, the hypodermics were less frequent. They were willing to let her do what she wanted, knowing among themselves that she could not live long.

Dan was having people in again to distract her, so she would think she was improving. He talked of spring when she would be out in the garden. She had believed it all until last night when Stanton Keith looked so guilty and bolted out of her room after he'd told her about the woman with cancer. She and the woman were parallel cases! And afterwards, Dan had watched her so carefully while he talked.

She wondered how long she would live. She felt too strong to die.

It was strange for her to be thinking like this so coldly about herself. She wasn't crying now; she had cried last night. Always ever since she was married, Dan had shared her thinking so completely. She had not been interested in illness except to know that Dan had cured this one or that. "Did the man get better?" she had used to ask briefly, warmed and secure if Dan said, "Much better, you should see him now"; or chilled and saddened if Dan said, "No, it didn't do any good, he's going out"; but saddened only momentarily as by a wind's swift passing across still water, her mind already gone on to something else. How unfeeling she had been!

Why hadn't Dan shared this thing with her? She wouldn't have minded so much as she did finding out this way. If she could feel that there were some small chance, but she couldn't. There was no use asking Dan.

Jean came running up the stairs. "Sue, don't sit in here in the dark. Heavens!" She went around the room, turning on lights, making soft circles of radiance that fell on her as she walked across the rug.

"I was watching the snow," Sue said and she was surprised that she could speak so calmly.

"It's really amounting to something. It's above the tops of your goloshes now. I'm glad we're having a party tonight; it will be good for Dan."

"Yes," Sue answered.

"Only, are you sure it isn't tiring for you, Sue? Everyone always wants to come up to see you if we'll let them, and Dan wants to have cocktails up here."

"I don't mind"; she couldn't keep from adding, "of course, they're just being kind."

"Nonsense, Sue. People ask about you everywhere I go. Do you like this or shall I wear that black dress?" Jean was switching to a safer topic.

"Do you want MacLean to fall more in love with you than he is now?" Sue made an effort to be light. "Tell Agnes to dress up, her husband's coming over too, and she doesn't need her uniform," Sue said slowly. She was playing a part; Jean didn't know that she knew.

"There, that's Dan! You feel equal to having them all up here, first, don't you?"

"Oh, yes." Suddenly, irrationally, Sue did want them. She wanted the laughter and talk and smoke right here, not coming up from below, muted.

The room was crowded, full of smoke and laughter. Sylvia Kaplan stood beside Sue's couch.

"I hear you like music, Mrs. Norton," Sylvia was saying.

She had once, but that seemed a long time ago. "Very much," she managed to say.

"I have a new album of Beethoven I'd like to bring over some afternoon and play for you. Would it tire you?"

"Thank you, I'd like it; I get very tired of the radio." Everyone wanted to do something for her, knowing that she would never be any better.

Then Peter Whitney stood by her, sipping his Scotch and soda, smiling at her and all the chatter. He didn't try to talk to her, but his standing there was a friendly gesture. He made her think of Dan. She looked across the room.

". . . If the same types went into politics that go into medicine we'd have a different brand of statesmanship!" Dan was saying.

"Spare us," Peter spoke up. "I can't think of a worse punishment than to be in politics."

"That's just the point," Dan went on. "But you took

a lot of drudgery and scutwork as a matter of course in medicine, and a good man would have to do the same in politics. We need more good men who feel they have a real call to politics, men who would make it their religion as you boys do your medicine."

"You mean we try to make medicine our religion," Bernard Kaplan interrupted quickly.

Dan smiled and sat back to listen. He loved to start arguments with a few speculative remarks.

"Medicine lets you down a little too often with the things it can do nothing about to make it a satisfactory religion," Kaplan observed quietly. "With some diseases still you might just as well turn medicine-man and dance yourself so tired you can't think any more."

Something uncomfortable had slipped into the atmosphere. Stanton Keith looked quickly over at Sue; Sue met his glance. Stan looked away again.

For a second, the room, the people in it, Dan's voice were blotted out. By the way Stanton's glance burned into her she knew that she had still been hoping. She had been dramatizing herself, telling herself that she was like a woman in childbirth, toying with the idea of incurability, bemusing herself with the snow, but all the time she had been hoping. The uncomfortable atmosphere in the room, Stanton Keith's glance snipped off that hope as neatly as she used to snip the first growth of delphiniums.

They were all talking again; people who were well could never talk of uncomfortable things longer than a second. Why didn't she tell them all that she knew? that she had known all along; they hadn't fooled her; Dan, Jean, any of them. She would be dramatic about it and say, "I'm one of those hopeless cases medicine can't do anything about."

"Mrs. Norton, your tray is coming right up; are you hungry?" Agnes bent over her. Sue noticed irrelevantly that Agnes looked like someone else out of her uniform, not so pretty, a little uncomfortable in a dress that was home-made.

"No, I'm not hungry."

They were all drifting out to the hall now, on their way downstairs. Dinner was ready for them down in the dining-room. Mrs. Norton would be uncomfortable having them around while she ate so awkwardly, poor thing. This conveyed by significant, well-meaning glances or the well-bred absence of them. Suddenly, unaccountably, she began to laugh.

"There, Mrs. Norton," Agnes spoke in a quiet voice that seemed to clothe her again in her stiff white uniform.

"Sue, dear," Dan came back from the hall, "I'm sorry. There was too much racket in here, wasn't there?" His hand was comforting.

But even though Dan smiled, his fingers were on her pulse and she could see his eyes going over her clinically. Why hadn't he told her? She hardened her heart against him. She stopped laughing, but she was not comforted. She was not deceived. The laughter had been none of her doing. It was involuntary. It had gone out of her now. She leaned back, tired. Obediently, she took the capsule Agnes brought her.

"Rest a while, dear; don't bother about dinner just now." Dan kissed her gently. "All right?"

She nodded, not looking at him. His hand tightened on hers, then he went out of the room. She heard his feet on the stairs.

Agnes sat down beside her.

"No, I want you to go on." Her words slurred more after the fit of laugher. Agnes mustn't stay. Agnes was dressed up in her bright blue dress piped in scarlet, the mark of an iron on the sleeve, where it had been pressed inexpertly. Agnes must go downstairs with Tom and the others. She didn't want anybody with her but Dan. But Agnes stayed with her until Dan came back up.

"Sue, drink this hot milk, dear." He sat down on the edge of the couch while she sipped it. Each sip trickled warmly down through her. Dan didn't tip the glass enough. With her tongue she held off the scum that was forming over the milk. The milk was comforting.

PART TWO

"Indeed, though in a wilderness, a man is never alone because he is with himself and his own thoughts."

". . . did we seriously perpend that one simile of St. Paul, 'Shall the vessel say to the Potter, "Why hast thou made me thus?"' it would prevent these arrogant disputes of reason."

Sir Thomas Browne
Religio Medici

DAN stood on the steps of the hospital. He smiled to see the Whitneys' old Ford rattling down the street. It made a ridiculous amount of noise getting under way and then chugged off smoothly enough. He breathed in the cold air and felt for his pipe.

"Good evening, Dr. Norton."

Dan turned to nod to Bernard Kaplan.

"I wanted to ask you about that case on six that died today, or will you be at the autopsy?"

Dan hesitated. He hadn't meant to. He hadn't been attending autopsies lately, but Kaplan seemed so eager.

"Yes, I thought I'd do it myself. It's an interesting case."

Kaplan's dark young face brightened. Dan had an instant's urge to keep him there with him.

"I phoned Jean to come over for me; if you'll wait, I'll give you a lift home," Dan offered.

"Thanks, Dr. Norton, Sylvia's waiting for me, I think. There she is." At that moment there were three staccato taps of a horn from a car along the curb.

When the Kaplans had gone, the curb directly in front of the entrance was bare. Dan disliked waiting alone tonight. The air that had seemed refreshing at first was sharp. It chilled him. For some minutes no one came in or out. He watched several cars turn the corner, but they only increased their speed and disappeared down the street.

He had just come from listening to Hutchins discuss the next year's appointments and the approaching battle with the regents. Drisco had come up to make a great fuss about a new record form, a blue card instead of a pink one, with new classifications . . . all of it so unimportant. The minutiae of the hospital world that had so absorbed him once seemed slipping from his focus of interest.

This morning when he had talked with the Hubbard family about their daughter with the malignant high blood pressure pity had filled his mind, and a pneumonia case on the ward had occupied him. But for the rest he had felt only a weary indifference. Looking back on his day now a wave of dissatisfaction washed up over his mind leaving it muddy.

In the old days, if his work ever lost its hold on him he used to call Sue and close up his desk for the afternoon and the two of them would drive off into the country, or into Chicago, to see a play. Sue's excited pleasure at the unexpected spree always took away any feeling of dullness.

Why didn't Jean come? He might better go in and dictate the letter he had left till tomorrow. To be caught like this and forced to wait by himself left him a prey to the miasma of his own thoughts.

A flock of student nurses came out the front door like children escaping from school. Their excited voices broke off to call out a respectful greeting to him and then went on. One of them burst into a high shriek of laughter that cut sharply in on his thoughts. He winced at the sound. He could hear again Sue's fit of laughter the other night. The remembrance sickened him as the sound had then.

There was no reason why he should have been so shocked at her outbreak. Unmotivated crying or laughing was part of the general instability occasioned by the disease, but it took seeing Sue, seeing her face laughing while her eyes remained mirthless and bewildered, to make him realize how hopeless her condition was. It was as though he had never touched sickness before.

He had always thought of himself as understanding and sympathetic. Hopeless situations and suffering had always moved him, but he realized that he had never really suffered any personal agony, even when his voice was most sympathetic, his hands most reassuring. Just as he had never been really bothered by the physical state of some of the dispensary patients who came in dirty and ragged, reeking of garlic or whiskey or body stench because he could feel at the same time his own bathed body in its clean linen separate from them. But he would never be so remote again now that he knew suffering so close at hand, almost in his own body; in his own life. . . .

A car turned the corner, slackened its speed. That was Jean.

"Hello, Dan. I'm sorry to be so late, but I ran up to tell Sue I was going for you."

"How did she seem today?"

"Well, it's been such a gloomy day, I think that depressed her."

He nodded and was silent. Jean wondered impatiently why she always brought Sue into the conversation immediately, as though some inner compulsion turned her words.

"I'll have to eat right away; I promised I'd go back over for an autopsy tonight."

"Oh, Dan, I wish you wouldn't go back tonight."

"I haven't been getting around to the autopsies as often as I should. I don't know . . ." He left his sentence unfinished. But it was a rest to sit beside Jean and let her drive. When he looked at her small, expressive face he forgot for a moment Sue's slackened features. There was enough resemblance between them to suggest Sue; but Jean was different. Jean was more restless than Sue. She turned and grinned at him so impishly she made him think of Donna.

Dan dragged himself back over to the hospital after dinner. He was too tired to do an autopsy; there was no real need of his doing it, Simms would have done it if he hadn't offered. Of course, he had always said that when a man got to the place where he didn't bother with autopsies he was slipping, but he didn't really care.

The sharp smell of formaldehyde came out to him as he turned down the corridor. The familiar smell stirred his senses. Automatically his mind dropped off its own problems, preparing for the thing at hand.

His instructors were already there in the postmortem room. Two or three students were sitting in the first row of raised seats. There was a girl among them, at her first autopsy, he judged by the set look of her face. Under the glare of the powerful drop-light lay the body, still covered over by a sheet. It was all so familiar he had no need to look around the room.

He nodded to them and to the quiet old man who stood by the table. "Good evening, Robbie."

Dan could never be quite sure, but he always thought he detected a flicker of amusement in the respectful expression of the assistant's face. Robbie had been there when he had done his first autopsy. Dan still remembered the suggestions Robbie had murmured to help him through it. "Saw way through the bone there, first, Doctor. . . ."

Perhaps it was old Robbie's presence that reminded him so vividly of any of a dozen autopsies when he was a student watching from the raised benches, arguing as Stan and Peter and Bernard were. These boys even looked like his own contemporaries. Tom, frowning to himself, reminded him of . . . but the name of the man had slipped his mind.

Robbie took away the sheet. Dan was always conscious of the nice air of dignity the old man had with the dead. It had its own quiet influence on the most callow student who tried to talk carelessly of stiffs and cadavers. Robbie tied Dan's gown for him while he pulled on his gloves.

"I was telling Stan, Dr. Norton, that the body shows

more wasting than you ever see from an ordinary stomach ulcer, isn't that so?" Peter asked.

"Remember how Gandhi's looked for years!" Dan said drily. "Do you boys have bets on what we'll find here?"

"Cancer of the bowel," Peter said firmly.

Stanton's judgment came more slowly. "I still think it's a stomach ulcer with obstruction." Bernard nodded in agreement. Tom had not seen the case on the ward.

"I suppose that it's not so simple as either one of you think," Dan said. "In fact, I suspect, gentlemen . . ." he could hear his voice assuming the tone and inflection of an old professor of his own student days . . . "that we'll find two distinct lesions here."

Dan glanced at old Robbie, knowing that he ventured diagnoses to himself sometimes that were uncannily accurate.

"If I'm right, all bets are off, but you'll both owe Robbie the price of a good cigar," Dan said as he made the long primary incision. He began dictating the details of the findings to the student who stood ready to take notes. Throughout the long teaching autopsy he was oblivious to everything except the clear and proper demonstration of the changes made by disease in the organs and tissues. He was too absorbed until after he was through to take any personal satisfaction in finding the two distinct lesions that he had predicted. It was good to work for a time on a body that could no longer suffer.

He had meant to leave as soon as he had demonstrated the pathology responsible for the symptoms, but he lingered, enjoying the discussion.

"I'm hungry, let's get something to eat," Tom suggested as they left the building.

Dan laughed. "Eat, drink and be merry. . . ."

"Sure, he wants to fatten up that precious body of his while there's still time," Stan said.

"Come on over to my house and I'll uncork some Scotch a G.P. up on six private gave me," said Peter.

"I'll stop long enough to have a short one with you," Dan said.

"Bless the grateful patients, may their tribe increase!" Tom intoned solemnly.

"I don't seem to have unearthed any of those G.P.'s to date," Bernard complained.

"Well, my boy, it takes a certain technique, but you keep on trying . . ." Peter told him in a patronizing voice. Bernard rammed Peter's hat over his face. They scuffled a minute and fell behind the others.

"Cut it out; Dan'll be waiting for us," Peter gasped.

"Weren't you surprised to have Dan show up at the post?" Bernard asked. "I expected to have old Simms there."

"Dan hasn't been to any this fall, has he?"

"Did you read that paper of his in the last *Annals?*"

"Yes," Peter answered. "It didn't have the Master's touch, if that's what you mean."

"You should have heard Ridley growl about it. He

said something about Dan's slipping, then he seemed to remember I was around and muttered that Dan was awfully harassed these days."

"I suppose doing all that work on arthritis that he did and then finding someone ahead of you on it wouldn't spur you on exactly. But it sure makes a difference in what you get out of an autopsy when Dan does it," Peter said.

"Pretty keen the way he summed up the possibilities right at the start!"

"He's the best of the whole bunch as a diagnostician; that's really why I came back here this year, just to get the work with Dan," Peter said, lowering his voice as they caught up with the others.

2

THE Whitneys moved into the old Lowery house today," Jean said. She and Dan were sitting in the library after dinner. In a minute Dan would go up to be with Sue. She wanted fiercely to hold him here a little longer with any casual triviality she could summon.

"That so?" Dan answered over his pipe-stem. "That's an old barracks of a place. What possessed them to move over there?"

"The rent's very low," Elsa said. "I saw her downtown yesterday and she was bubbling with excitement."

Why did she have to resort to some news about the young group for conversation? Yet Dan seemed interested and she made the most of it.

Dan shook his head and smiled. The financial wrigglings of the young faculty were always amusing. He and Sue had been pinched those first years. You couldn't get away from your youth in this place. It kept returning to you in the new crop of youngsters always around the University.

"What's Whitney's wife like?" he asked unexpectedly.

"Quite nice, on the serious side; misses studying and that sort of thing, terribly in love. Peter keeps cropping up in her conversation," Jean told him.

Dan chuckled. "That's proper." He rose and went on upstairs. Sue had been like that, too.

Jean sat a minute in front of the fire. Then she glanced out the window at the dark. She hadn't heard Donna come in, she remembered guiltily. She went out on the porch, bareheaded, without a coat, liking the freezing air that stung her face and arms and legs. It was clear tonight, but little drifts from yesterday's snow held along the porch, frozen where they had blown into some semblance of a relief map.

"Donna!" Jean called out, feeling her voice shrill and unpleasant. She wondered if it rose to Dan and Sue sitting upstairs. She went down the walk toward the driveway. Donna knew better than to stay out after dark. She called again.

"Donna, you must not go out after dinner!" she said sharply when Donna came; the more sharply because something in the act mocked at her. It had a kind of familiarity about it. She remembered her mother calling Sue in from play. Sue had been older and stayed out after she did. She was always ready for bed before Sue came in and she had used to envy Sue. Perhaps she had always envied her until now.

Dan sat reading aloud. Sue lay very quietly with her face on her hand, watching him. He looked up from his page and met her eyes.

"What, dear?"

She shook her head and he went on, but he no longer heard the words he read. When Agnes came to tell him there was a call from the hospital he went gladly, not proud of the relief he felt.

Jean was in the library as he came through the hall.

"I have to drop over to the hospital for a few minutes, Jean, do you want to drive over with me?"

"I'd love to," Jean said simply. She went quickly to get her coat and neither she nor Dan spoke until they were down the drive. The evening that had lain like slack yarn across her knees was pulled tight.

"Where's MacLean tonight, Jean?" he began teasingly.

"I don't know," Jean answered, watching the road. She wished Dan wouldn't take that older brother tone with her.

She looked out at the lighted fraternity houses as they drove past. There was a dance in the big house on the corner. The door stood wide open as though it were not mid-winter. That was the way life should be, thrown open extravagantly to love, not kept tightly closed over a secret as hers was. The music came out to them across the snow-covered lawn. Dan drove more slowly.

There was an edge to her voice when she spoke.

"Your call wasn't an emergency then?"

But if Dan noticed it he gave no sign. "There's no hurry; an old fellow in his seventies, old Talbot Stevenson. I gather he's a hopeless case. I'm just going over to see that he's comfortable."

Jean glanced at Dan. He spoke so calmly of the seventies, of dying.

"But he's been quite a figure in his day," Dan went on. "I don't suppose he's ready to call it quits even yet."

Why should he be, Jean wondered. Sickness and death came on you before you had had enough of life; when you still wanted so much. Dan talked about them too easily.

"Dan, no one ever is."

"I wonder if Sue isn't sometimes. Jean, you don't think I should tell Sue how hopeless her condition is, do you?"

"Oh, no, Dan." Jean was shocked. "What possible good could that do?"

"I know . . . but perhaps a person has a right to know. Sue always faced things pretty well. When she knew she could never have a child . . ."

"That's different, Dan; some things, but not that! Would you want to know?"

"Yes," Dan said slowly. "Yes, I think I should; what about you?"

"If I knew I couldn't get any better—" Jean looked off across the lighted houses—"I'd get in all I could before it was over," she said vehemently, "the way they said soldiers did before a big offensive. I'd buy gorgeous clothes and fly to Europe . . . nothing would bother me. I'd go around feeling so superior to all the people around me who were worried about staying within their budgets and their silly little lives . . ." Jean had forgotten all about Sue.

Dan laughed. "I believe you would, Jean. The trouble is that Sue won't go out in a day or a month. It may be a long-drawn-out affair. You can't stay on that high crest over a stretch like that. And Sue isn't very pagan," he added thoughtfully.

Dan got out in front of the hospital. "I won't be long."

When he came back out, Jean had shucked down in her seat, her collar up around her ears.

"Get cold?"

She shook her head. "Just lonely, Dan. You left on a bad note," she laughed. "I don't suppose you and Sue know what loneliness is, you've always been so close."

"I suppose that's right, but I know now. Sue seems to grow more remote all the time."

"Agnes said she's going to try to get her interested in arranging scrap books. She thinks Sue could do that."

Dan's mouth compressed into a thinner line. It hurt him to think of Sue reduced to doing busy work.

"Tell Agnes I wouldn't push it if she doesn't want to," Dan muttered. He let the car move slowly along the frozen street.

"Dan, let's drive out the state highway? I love driving at night. When Sidney flew the night mail plane I was nicer to him, I think."

She rarely mentioned her first marriage. Dan was surprised to hear her now. "Did you ever fly with him?"

"No, Sidney couldn't take anyone with the mail, but I used to watch for his lights going overhead. I could see them from the apartment window. That was it, I suppose. When he was flying I thought of him as different, rather splendid, then he'd come home and sink into a chair with the newspaper and drink too much and we'd jangle so about little things . . . it isn't very good taste to talk about him now. It's like talking about the dead." She wished she hadn't mentioned Sidney and yet she wanted to talk to Dan about herself.

"He must miss you and Donna, though, after having you."

Jean shrugged. "I don't believe he does. He's married again, you know. You shouldn't be able to live with a person seven years, or even at all, and not have it change you, unless you're just a sensualist, of course; do you think, Dan?" Her voice was suddenly wistful.

Dan was silent, thinking of himself and Sue. He could hardly remember when his life was separate from Sue's. Now that she was sick, he felt lost. He had depended on her without knowing it.

"But those seven years didn't change me," Jean said, "unless they made me bitter and a lot older. I was lonely all through them." She wanted to ask Dan if he thought she was very much changed from the younger sister he remembered, but she was still.

It was a relief to talk with Jean, Dan thought. Sue's silences seemed to drain him of anything to say. There were so many things he tried to avoid mentioning, now that Sue was sick. He hadn't talked like this since his twenties. He remembered pouring out his ideas and aims to Sue, then; but after they were married he had been wrapped up in Sue, interested in ideas, in his work. She understood him so well without many words.

When Sue's sickness had descended, it seemed to him that his emotions were as benumbed as some region of the body made insensate by a local anesthetic. Talking with Jean like this stirred those benumbed emotions uncomfortably. The return to feeling was painful, but it was more like living than the numbed state he had been in.

"We'll drive over to Bennett and back; that's thirty

miles," Dan said. "I'll go past Whitneys' first and ask Peter to drop over to see my patient if the hospital calls. You said the Whitneys had already moved into the Lowery house, didn't you?"

When they came to the Lowery house the curtains were not drawn. They could see the wavering reflection of fire-light in the front room.

"I'll wait for you out here, Dan; you won't be but a minute."

"Oh, no, come in and see them."

"I don't want to, Dan, please; not this time."

Dan went up the walk to the prim old entrance alone. Of a sudden, without reason, she didn't want to go in there. She and Dan had never been so close before. It would spoil it to go in and be casual; to say, "Dan had to go to the hospital so I tagged along." She sat in the car watching the lighted window.

She saw Peter cross the room to answer Dan's ring. Dan passed in front of the window. He had kept on his overcoat. Elsa came over to the table to turn on a light. They were all laughing. It was queer to look in like this without hearing what they were saying. She had always been looking in at Sue and Dan's life like this; but now she was in the room with Dan and Sue was upstairs, sick.

The thought took Jean's eyes away from the window. The darkness, lighted only by infrequent lampposts and the snow-covered lawns, was a relief. She followed the curve of an iron fence until it broke off at a driveway. Dan was lonely, too. Sue was too sick to care. People were cowards with each other; afraid to speak their hearts. They just drifted, fumbling through trivialities toward understanding, missing it because of their cowardice. She wouldn't be like that. She would speak out. She sat in the dark, squeezing her hands tightly together.

Elsa and Peter had been sitting by the fire when Dan rang.

"Am I your first visitor?" Dan called from the doorway.

"Oh, Dr. Norton, come in by the fire," Elsa urged. "We're gloating over a real fireplace." Elsa crossed to the table to turn on a light.

"I can only stay a minute. You look as though you had always lived here."

"You should have seen us this afternoon! Peter said the house reminded him of the House of Usher and he expected it to fall on us, and the furnace smoked and the rooms looked so big and dingy I thought I'd gotten us into a terrible mess. The place just seemed hopeless," Elsa said.

"I remember it as a very cheerful place," Dan told her. "When the Lowerys lived here, Sue and I used to come over often. Let's see, I was a junior instructor then; we must have been about your ages. This house has seen plenty of good living and I'm sure there are no ghosts."

Elsa laughed. "I love it now. After Peter built the fire it was all right."

"But she gets all the credit for seeing the possibilities in the old place. She rented it on her own hook," Peter said.

Their evident satisfaction with each other amused Dan but they made him feel his age. He sat there warming himself at their fire, listening to them talk about the house. They reminded him of Sue and himself again.

"Oh, Dan, that diabetic coma on my ward cleared up nicely," Peter said irrelevantly.

Peter was as he had been. His interest in his work underlay every part of his life and bubbled up unexpectedly like a spring cropping out all through a meadow. It didn't pay. About all his own interest had done was to dilute some of his care-free happiness with worry and it had made him no better able to cure Sue now.

"Pretty to see him snap out of it!" Peter went on about his diabetic.

Peter's remark brought him back to the purpose of his call. Dan nodded. "I'm just back from the hospital, Peter. Old Talbot Stevenson came in. He's one of the regents, you know. He can't get well, but he came out here as a last hope. I have to be out of reach of the phone until late tonight so I wanted you to be on tap if his special nurse calls." Dan stood up to go. He had seemed in a hurry when he came, Elsa thought. Now he hesitated almost as though he hated to leave.

"Good night; the best of luck to your new house!" he said to Elsa. It was no wonder that Peter adored him. They both went with him to the door. Elsa glanced out before she turned off the porch-light.

"Why, Peter, Jean was in the car all the time! Wasn't it queer that she didn't come in?" As the car passed under the street lamp they could see two heads against the back window. "They're always together so I can't understand why . . ."

"It was nice to have Dan stop in," Peter cut in on her unspoken thought.

"Oh, Peter," Elsa murmured contritely, slipping her hand in his arm. She let her sentence go unfinished, but when they were sitting in front of the fire her thoughts went back to the silhouette of the two heads in the car. Out of a long silence she said abruptly, "Peter?"

"What?" Peter anwered sleepily from where he lay on the rug.

"Would you keep on loving me if I were like Mrs. Norton?"

"What do you think, Foolish?" He reached over and pulled off her slipper. "Let's go to bed before you go morbid on me."

"Are they pleased with their new quarters?" Jean asked as they drove away.

"Yes, I think they are. As you said, they're absorbed in each other; it's easy to see that. They struck me as being quite . . . adequate to life." He was silent as they drove down through the main street, past the dark shops and movies and turned away from the residence section. Jean waited. She thought his mind had gone on to something else when he said, "That's the feeling I've lost hold of these last few months."

"Why do you say that, Dan? It isn't so. You're the most adequate person I know."

"No, I'm not, really. Things have gone pretty well for me, that's all; until now." He drove for a block or more, then he said, glancing at her, "Keep thinking I am, Jean, that'll help."

She didn't speak, hoping he would go on. She did mean something to Dan! He needed her, aside from having her run the house and keep the atmosphere cheerful.

"You know, the two of them remind me of Sue and myself about the time we first came here," Dan went on in a different tone. It was an effort for Jean to come back to the Whitneys.

"Dan, you were never like Peter Whitney; he's such a serious young man," Jean objected.

"Oh, I was serious, too, Jean, stupidly so. You

didn't know me well then, and such a confident young fool!" The self-mockery in Dan's tone was sharper than the rime that collected along the windshield.

All of Jean's carefully thought-out sentences vanished from her mind as completely as the white smoke of her breath against the cold air. This wasn't the time, but she could wait. She touched Dan's elbow. "It's later than I thought, Dan. Let's turn back."

Dan looked at his watch. "It is late; I'll turn around."

He went back up past the old Lowery house on Delancey Street instead of turning over on Hanover. As they went past the house, Dan said,

"I wondered if they were still up gloating over their first fireplace."

3

DAN was called to the hospital again after dinner. That was the way with a case like Talbot Stevenson's, the family expected you there by the bedside the whole time: the family needed as much attention as the patient, he stormed humorously to Sue. Once, Sue would have scolded him for a remark like that, or made fun of him, but tonight she seemed not to have heard it. She lay watching him without speaking.

"I'll answer all the family's questions and then I'll be back, Sue." He tried to keep his tone light.

"Good-by, Dan," she answered thickly.

On the main floor of the hospital he met Peter Whitney.

"Hello, Peter," Dan nodded. Then he noticed that Peter looked ill at ease, almost embarrassed.

"Dr. Norton," Peter began formally, like an intern reporting a case on a ward round, "Mr. Stevenson is semi-comatose now; I've just come from there." He seemed to hesitate.

Dan nodded. "The transfusion this noon couldn't do much good, of course. I had it done more for Mrs. Stevenson's sake so she would feel that we were doing everything possible." Dan was aware of the tightening of Peter's face; the same look he had noticed this noon when he dropped in and ordered the transfusion. "You understood that, didn't you, Peter? There are times when it's a kindness to treat the relatives as well as the patient. Perhaps I made a little too much fuss up there this noon. But you knew I felt you had done everything that was really necessary."

Peter looked back at Dan steadily. "I see. It did rather make it look as though, if I'd had my wits about me, I should have ordered one before. But it wasn't that so much . . ." Peter didn't finish his sentence.

Dan waited. "As what?" he prompted.

Peter flushed. "Well, the old fellow was going out peacefully enough; it seemed cruel and unnecessary to prolong his sufferings and the family's. It seemed a little . . ." Peter brought the word out with an effort . . . "melodramatic for you."

Dan hesitated. Even yet he didn't take criticism well, he never had. There was no reason why he should explain his orders to this young whelp, but no irritation showed in his voice.

"Perhaps the truth of the matter is, Peter, that the last year has given me such a taste of the relatives' point of view that I think of them more than I used to." The grim humor of that truth left his lips twisted a little. He saw Peter's instant response.

"I see, Dan," Peter said. "I'm sorry."

"Come back up with me, Peter, and we'll have a look at him again," Dan said, brushing the whole thing aside.

"He's a fine old man," Peter commented.

The admitting desk called up about an emergency admission while Dan was still with Talbot Stevenson.

"Come along, Peter," Dan said. "It's a heart case."

They met the stretcher as they got off at the fourth floor. A shabby, anxious woman walked by the stretcher. Her eyes besought Dan's as she stood outside the door of the room. She kept fastening and unfastening her handbag with red, nervous fingers. Again, there was the family to complicate the care of the patient, Dan thought. He had never been so conscious of families before.

Peter stood beside the bed while Dan made the examination, but he listened to the heart sounds for himself. The man was a laborer, about fifty. His skin was grotesquely pale under a coat of grime. The hand nearest to Dan was square, powerful, checked with black, black-nailed; the hand of a man who had had no truck with sickness before now, Dan thought.

"We'll have that pain fixed in a few minutes," Dan spoke reassuringly to him. The man's eyes responded but in the grip of his pain he made no attempt to answer.

"Well?" Dan asked as they walked down the hall to the nurses' station.

"Acute cardiac infarction and he looks pretty darn sick."

Dan nodded. "The outlook is bad, but we'll do what we can." He was glad that the woman with the pocketbook seemed to have disappeared for the moment. He wrote out the usual orders and arranged for special care.

"The patient's wife said they wanted to keep expenses down as much as they could, Dr. Norton," the night supervisor told him.

"Charge it to me, then; I want special care for him tonight."

"I'll be glad to stay with him, Dan," Peter put in. "I'd like to for my own interest."

"All right, Peter; it won't do you any harm. I'll be over about midnight to see Stevenson again; I'll look in on you. If he goes out before that, call me."

"Dan, why wouldn't this be a good time to try that

radical treatment Hughes reported at the Journal Club?"

Dan shook his head. "No, I don't think so, Peter; as I said then, there are so many things against it."

"Even in what looks like a terminal case? The article reported ten cases with good results," Peter urged.

"Let them report more than that before you try it on your patients, Peter. I don't believe it's sound. Well, good night."

Peter was disappointed. He wished Dan would discuss the treatment with him, but he had so definitely closed the matter. His tone was almost oracular. Peter went back to the patient.

Dan was glad that the emergency case had come up. Peter had been hurt about the transfusion evidently, but taking him up to see the new case would restore his *amour propre*. He was pleased that Peter wanted to stay with the patient; that was the sort of thing he would have jumped at himself, once. He must tell Sue about it.

Then his thoughts came to a sudden standstill. His mind was like a dog, trained to bring home every morsel it found, that goes on by habit after his master is gone and the house left vacant. That was the way he felt about Sue. Every colorful happening he saved to tell Sue, but when he told it to her she seemed hardly interested any more.

Sue had changed mentally. He had noticed it ever

since the night she had burst out laughing. And Jean said she seemed hurt at all manner of little things. She didn't try to talk as much. When he was with her, her eyes were always on him but she shook her head when he asked her playfully what she was thinking.

And she had lost all interest in going downstairs. Whenever he suggested it she turned away from the idea sharply. It was hard to get her to exert herself. Her trip down to hear him must have exhausted her more than they realized.

At his own door he wondered why he had not stayed over at the hospital, himself, instead of coming home.

The house was dark except for the light in the hall. Agnes came to tell him Sue was asleep.

"Where's Mrs. Keller?" Dan asked.

"She went out with Dr. MacLean," Agnes said.

Dan went into the library. He counted on finding Jean here in the evenings. He got out the outline of the paper he had promised the *Maryland Research Journal* for June and glanced over it. The silence of the house distracted him more than any noise could. He forced his attention to follow the pages he had written. Then he bundled the whole sheaf of papers into an envelope, and sat idle and alone in front of his own fire. He still had a couple of months' grace on that paper. He wondered if Jean were interested in MacLean.

When he went back over to the hospital he was aware how little he had been over here at night this last year. Since Sue's illness everybody tried to spare him more; perhaps he spared himself.

He liked seeing the out-patient benches empty of patients. All the dust of the day was obliterated. The linoleum floor shone wetly from its nightly scrubbing. From one of the corridors came the swishing sound of a vacuum cleaner. He pushed open the swinging doors into the general waiting room. On the wicker settee a woman was lying asleep, her head on her pocketbook. She looked vaguely familiar as he glanced at her. Then he remembered that she was the shabby woman who had walked by the stretcher.

The quiet tonight seemed intense. The only sounds were those of his own feet, subdued by the cork flooring. He could hear the wind blowing around the corner of the hospital and the irrelevant, cheerful gurgling of a water cooler.

This wing of the hospital was new since his own days as an instructor, yet he seemed to remember these same sounds; the same heavy quiet, even the startling noise of his own footsteps going down a corridor when he had been alone at night on some emergency.

He opened the door of the room softly. Peter was sitting by the bed, but he came out to the hall at once when he saw Dan.

"Dan, I believe he's going to make it!" Even his low tone of voice could not suppress his eagerness.

"Good; I really didn't think he would."

Peter hesitated. "I don't know what you'll think,

Dan, but he was slipping all the time so . . . so I took a chance and tried the radical treatment. I know you practically ordered me not to. The nurse was shocked at the unusual orders but I told her I'd take the full responsibility." Peter rubbed his ear in his embarrassment. He frowned as he spoke. He was putting it very badly.

At first Dan hadn't quite heard him right. As he realized that Peter had gone directly against his advice on the case he caught his lip between his teeth in a way he had.

"I forget that your generation missed out on the army entirely," he said.

Peter flushed. "The man looks fifty per cent better right now," he insisted stubbornly.

"Well, let's see him," Dan said, moving down the hall ahead of Peter. Dan was irritated. He took himself in hand as he went; mustn't be like old Adair who wouldn't try insulin . . . but Peter was wrong in going against his advice; perhaps the independence he had liked in him was plain conceited rashness. . . .

Dan took Peter's chair by the bedside. The man stirred and Dan bent over him so closely he was merged with him. His breathing was easier, more regular, Peter was right about that. Once the man muttered unintelligible words. Then the room was still except for his breathing and the slight jarring of the rubber-stopped legs of Dan's chair.

Peter stood on the other side of the bed waiting.

Dan should be able to see for himself that the man was better. And he was failing rapidly before the orders were changed . . . that was clear enough from the chart. If Dan refused to admit it because he'd advised against the treatment . . . but he couldn't do that. Peter watched him anxiously.

Dan rose from his chair. There was no doubt about it; the man was better. For an instant he felt a twinge of envy at Peter's boldness, then it was effaced by satisfaction with the result and Peter. He looked across the bed and nodded.

"Mhmm," he grunted and Peter was satisfied.

Outside in the corridor Dan laid his hand on Peter's arm. "That's first-rate, Peter. You've shown me something." They went down through the hospital together, through the lobby where the woman lay sleeping. Dan nodded toward her.

"She ought to wake up and find her man better."

"Should," Peter said and grinned at Dan. The same elated feeling held them both.

"Well," Dan said, "feel pretty good?"

Peter grinned.

"I'll go on up and do what I can for Mrs. Stevenson. Good night, Peter."

Dan waited by the bed with Mrs. Stevenson until her husband had died. When he came down he was surprised and touched to find Peter sitting in the outer lobby.

"You shouldn't have waited for me, Peter."

"Oh, I haven't been sitting here long. I had to go up and see our cardiac once more. He looks still better. I'm sure he's going to make it now."

"You've done a nice job there, Peter."

"Thanks, I'd have been pretty sunk if it hadn't turned out all right."

"Well, it's been quite a night. Let's celebrate with a cup of coffee at Sweeney's," Dan suggested.

They walked over to the all-night restaurant thrashing out the principles of the treatment. The street was empty except for an occasional milk wagon or late car. The cemetery that spread with macabre humor between the hospital and the residence section lay somber in the darkness except where a white stone thrust its importunate face out of the shadow. But at the corner a neon sign spelled out "Sweeney's" in cheerful red letters. And through the frosted glass of the front window a pyramid of oranges gleamed warmly golden.

Dan felt curiously rested as he sat on the high stool at the lunch counter.

4

"OH, Dan, my hands shake so much, it's only a bore for the rest of you," Sue protested.

"You know that isn't so, Sue. I feel like playing, myself." Dan set up the card table as he spoke and moved it against Sue's couch.

"We've had some good times playing Russian Bank, haven't we, Mrs. Norton?" Agnes asked, smiling. She was wondering whether they would want her tonight or whether she would be free. She hadn't seen Tom all week, Mrs. Norton had seemed so poorly.

"Yes," Sue said, but so tonelessly the single word carried in it the monotony of the long afternoons.

"You know, Sue, we must take up chess again," Dan said. Sue watched him. When he was in high spirits like this she was drawn out of herself. All the last week he had seemed so far away from her. It had been easy to hold the secret of her incurability tightly to her, separating Dan from her because of it. She had blamed him for not telling her.

"Remember playing when it rained so much in Scotland, Sue?"

Sue's eyes remembered. How foolish she had been. Dan had not told her how sick she was because he couldn't do anything about it; because he felt too badly.

Dan turned to Agnes. "You go ahead, Agnes, we're going to play some bridge with Dr. MacLean and Mrs. Keller and then I'll help Mrs. Norton to bed."

"I'll be back early, Mrs. Norton; is there anything before I go?" Agnes asked tentatively.

"No, you needn't come back until morning," Sue said.

In her own room Agnes hurried out of her uniform. She was eager to be out of this house, tonight. The depressing weather of the last few days had weighed on her. Unless she did something with her, Mrs. Norton watched the snow or the fire and seemed to take little interest in anything, even reading. If she would just talk more, even in her slow, staggering speech, but she was so quiet.

Agnes shrugged off the burden of Mrs. Norton's illness as she powdered her nose. Going to a movie with Tom would fix her up. She had been here so steadily it was getting her down. It was always that way on a long case when she felt so sorry for the patient; it took it out of her. She wondered how long Mrs. Norton . . . she seemed at a standstill now.

"Jean, Mac!" Dan called downstairs. "Come up and we'll give you a trimming."

Dan's voice was just a shade too hearty, Sue thought; there was too much effort in it. She would rather have had Dan to herself all evening, but perhaps she was serious too much of the time, now. Mac and Jean wouldn't want to play; Jean never had liked bridge. "Bridge is so middle-aged," she used to say. But they were both coming, pretending to gaiety, making their voices eager. Had she always used to notice the tone of people's voices so carefully, or just since her own had lost all tone?

"So you think you'll beat us, Doctor?" Mac asked.

"Don't be intimidated, Mac, Dan doesn't even know the new scoring," Jean played up.

Sue smiled. "You're sure you don't mind?" But she was sorry she had said it the next minute; it took so long to say it; they were so quick to reassure her. How pretty Jean was tonight, so slim and vivid. Sue saw Mac's eyes on Jean, saw Jean meet his eyes and smile. She had come to watch people so much more closely.

Dan was shuffling for Sue. He picked up her cards so she wouldn't have to fumble for them.

Sue had a good hand. She almost let Mac have the bid for five hearts so she wouldn't have to play it, then she stiffened and bid five spades. Dan raised her to six. She leaned a little nearer to the table.

"Do you want another pillow, Sue?" Jean asked.

"I'm fine." She wished Jean wouldn't. She pinched the thin pasteboards between her finger-tips, the feeling in her fingers was so dulled. As her hand neared the table it shook even more than usual. Dan quietly took the tricks in for her.

"Smart lady!" Mac murmured approvingly at her finesse.

They were anxious to compliment her, so careful not to seem to see her slow, painful movements. When she played with Agnes the trembling of her hand was not so marked. She wanted to tell them that; to boast like a child.

In her distraction she lost count of the hearts; was the nine high? She must make this to show that she was as keen as ever. She was absurdly intent of a sudden. Hearts had been led three times . . . she forced her mind back. She couldn't think. She mustn't get so nervous. This was the way she had used to feel when she played in piano concerts as a child.

She took a chance. The nine was high; she made her six. She lay back on the couch and let her hands rest in her lap. She had always been rather good at games.

"Little slam!" Jean said.

"Of course, we always make a little or a big slam," Dan boasted.

Sue and Dan won that rubber and had a game on the second. She was enjoying it. When the clock on the mantel struck the half hour after ten she was surprised, the evening had gone so fast.

Suppose she could never get well, no one knew how long she could live! All week she had held the thought of incurability in her mind, making herself suck at it as she used to suck at a lemon when she was a child, to see how it made her lips pucker. She sat a little straighter, throwing the thought away.

"Double four no-trump!" she said almost gaily. It didn't matter that her hand jerked spasmodically when she laid down a card. There! they were set!

As she raised her eyes she saw Mac smothering a yawn. She glanced at Dan and Jean. They were sitting so silently, the expression on Dan's face was withdrawn. Jean was looking at her watch. She saw them suddenly as three adults who had been amusing a child for the evening. She had been the only one really engrossed. Perhaps they had even let her win. She wanted to drop the cards, to tell them it was no fun for her, either.

"Well, here's where we sew up this rubber," Dan said in a tone that was too hearty.

"Oh, I don't know about that! Don't count your chickens before they're hatched, darling!" Jean retorted.

"You'll have to work for it!" Mac warned.

Their conspiracy was so evident. Sue looked at her hand, it was good for a demand bid easily, but she said perversely, in a tone she thought of as bored, though it sounded like the rest of her words, "Pass."

Dan got the bid and she had to lay down her hand.

"Why, Sue, that's wonderful strength, why didn't you raise him?" Jean asked.

Dan looked at her searchingly. "Tired, dear?" he asked and the gentleness in his voice sent instant angry tears to her eyes. "We'll stop after this hand." He played it swiftly, expertly.

Mac wrote down the score and added it all up as though it mattered, as though anyone were interested any more.

"Well, you beat us by only two hundred and fifty points, even if you did win two rubbers," he announced.

"I call that a moral victory," Jean said in just the right tone of vivacity.

The trite words sounded hollow in Sue's ears. There

was something almost indecent about these casual remarks used to cover over their boredom.

"I'll go down and make you a hot toddy, Sue, and then tuck you in," Jean said in the tone of the capable, well person to an invalid. Sue hated it at the same time that she was ashamed of her own feeling.

"I must get back over to the hospital," Mac said. "Good night, Sue, we'll wallop you next time!" Mac was always agreeable. Sue smiled back without really wanting to.

Dan carried her back to bed. She never minded being dependent upon him. He had taken care of her before when she was sick. Dan was always more gentle than any nurse. As long as she did live she had Dan. That was enough. She would tell him that she knew about herself. He would comfort her.

But her face showed nothing of her thoughts. He couldn't get used to her with her hair short. Her face was fuller. She reached out to touch his arm and he took her hand to steady the awful jerking. He smiled with a conscious effort.

"We had a pretty good game," Dan said with that same false animation that brought back the picture of them to her: Mac smothering a yawn, Jean looking at her watch, Dan's face preoccupied. How clumsy she must have looked to them, grotesque, pathetic.

"I don't believe I care for bridge any more," Sue

answered perversely. She turned away when Dan kissed her.

"I want to see Stephen before I go to bed," Dan said.

Then Jean came up with the glass of hot milk and whiskey and Dan had gone. Sue sipped her milk with its half-sweet taste that was not unpleasant but yet a little medicinal. She felt it going down her throat making a spot of warmth that spread through her body.

"Good night, dear," Jean said. "I'll leave your door open and if you want anything, just ring your bell."

Dan walked in the direction of Stephen Ridley's as though he had some purpose. He felt he had to get out after the ordeal of playing bridge with Sue, keeping up a pretense of light-heartedness, sitting across the table waiting for Sue to put down a card, watching the awful jerking of her hands, listening to her slow, toneless voice.

Sue had lost ground a little; there was no mistaking that her mouth pulled down a trifle at the corner, her speech slurred more. She had played out of a heavy kind of impassivity. She had seemed to take a kind of childish pleasure in playing, but she was dulled. Afterwards, she had seemed almost petulant. She was growing childish.

He walked more briskly, trying to shake off his depression.

He wasn't finding satisfaction in his work. The work

this year irritated him at a dozen points. The whole world seemed sick sometimes. "We're all grossly pathologic!" Ridley always said. Lord, how true it was. What a fool a man was to put in his whole life with illness.

There was that case Peter Whitney had saved. That had shown him how dull he was growing. He had never used to be like that. He had always been ready to try a new treatment. Pretty soon he would be no fit teacher for young men. He would go the way of all the old fogeys.

And that paper for the *Maryland Research Journal*; he couldn't seem to get on with it. But with Sue lost to him like this he didn't really care.

Sue was gone from him more completely than if she were dead. Even her body that they tried so assiduously to preserve was not Sue's. Sue was always supple, quick-moving, slim. There was nothing of her left in the rigid, leaden-faced woman who had wearied of the game like a child. She used to be . . .

Now he was off. Thinking of Sue as she used to be, this time or that time, was an escape from the cruelty of the present as futile as drink. He knew it and went right on taking it.

There was the time he lost a pneumonia case. It must have been after they moved out on the river road because he remembered coming home late at night and Sue came down and unlocked the door and sat on the stairs in her nightgown to talk to him. Sue often did that, as though, they used to say, he were just calling and had to say good night in the hall.

He told her he'd lost the case. He'd felt pretty badly over it.

"But, Dan, you did everything you could."

"That's it, Sue. If I'd given the serum earlier I think now she might have made it." That fact had haunted him all the way home. "I thought of it, Sue, but . . ." He remembered walking up and down the hall explaining it all to her. Sue sat as solemn as any judge, letting him rail at himself without interrupting or excusing him, her eyes troubled at his suffering. He sat down beside her on the stairs, finally, talked out.

"I know, Dan," she said, simply. In sharing his doubts and self-blame she seemed to lift some of the load from him. The sharing changed nothing but it helped.

He had always told her all his mistakes and failures, even his doubts. It was no wonder that he was lost without her, he thought impatiently.

He came to Stephen's house and saw two cars parked out in front. Another night he would have gone in gladly to join in the good talk, but tonight he hesitated. Then he turned and went back to his own house as he had gone out, the color of his mood unchanged.

The house was warm, dark. There was a single light in front of the mirror in the hall. He took off his coat and hat and hung them up with slow, deliberate movements, tucking his scarf into one coat sleeve. Then he went out to the kitchen and poured himself a stein of beer. He took it into the library and sat down in his big chair. There were still a few red coals in the grate, but he didn't bother to knock them together or to turn on the lights. He sipped the beer, aware tonight of the metallic taste of the silver stein, of the cold running from the beaded tankard into his finger-tips. He was bemusing himself with safe, surface things, ridding himself of his thoughts for the night. But, in spite of himself, his mind dipped down in; finding loneliness and an obscure sense of failure.

"Dan!" Jean stood in the doorway. He had not even heard her coming. "I heard you come in, Dan. I came down to keep you company."

"Good, will you have some beer?"

Jean shook her head. She sat down on the stool in front of the fender, the dress or negligee she wore falling into soft folds around her. The light stuff took the red glow of the coals. She looked into the fire without speaking.

Then he felt her looking across at him. He picked up his stein without meeting her eyes. He hesitated even to speak. Jean had the power of creating an intimacy of atmosphere without any conscious effort. Tonight it enfolded them.

"The bridge was too much for me this time; I had to get out after it," he said finally.

"Yes," she said and met his eyes. They were silent again. He finished the stein of beer and set it over on the table. He leaned his head back against the chair and felt a loosening of some tension that had held him taut. A silence with Jean was a different thing from the awkward pauses that came with Sue. There was no need of pretending with Jean, no need of watching the conversation for fear of hurting her or bringing up things from the past that would make her remember other times.

"But, Dan, you mustn't let it throw you the way it has lately." Jean's voice was very low, as low as the fire. She stood up. He could just hear the soft resettling of the folds of her gown that was louder than the little sigh she gave. He had never thought of Jean as tired before. Life couldn't be easy for her either.

"Jean, you've had enough bad luck, you mustn't let our troubles depress you too much."

"Oh, Dan!" Her voice was quick in reproach. He couldn't see the expression of her face. It was only whiteness in the dark. "Dan, don't you know I want to be here with you?"

"I know it would be intolerable without you, Jean. You hold the place together," he said gently, standing beside her.

"Dan," Jean whispered. Her words came in a rush, breathlessly. "I couldn't be any place else because I love you." Her face was lifted toward him out of the darkness. She was young and well and alive. She was as Sue had been and yet not Sue. She loved him.

"Jean," he answered and kissed her forehead in a

sudden impulse of gratitude, but she forced her head back a little and he kissed her lips and felt hers seeking his. The warm dark was so still it seemed to hold them there together. A coal slipped through the grate and dropped into the open ashpit. A faint sound came back from its fall that was the measure of their silence.

He could feel her heartbeat and her breath and all her flesh and nerves responsive to him. He held her close. All the tension and dissatisfaction of the evening ebbed, leaving him free; free to take delight in the softness of her body against his, in her softly whispered words that neither dragged nor slurred but sang in the stillness, "I didn't mean to tell you, Dan"; in her face when she turned toward the coals' glow. He pressed his lips hard against hers.

"Dan, it can't hurt Sue."

He scarcely understood her words at first, he was so lost in feeling. Then he realized what she had said.

"No," he whispered back more slowly. "No, it can't hurt Sue." But the mention of Sue altered his free feeling. He thrust his hands awkwardly in his pockets and turned from her to the fire. He felt Jean waiting. Once he heard her catch her breath as though she were going to speak.

"Jean, you must go now," he said briefly, as he gave orders at the hospital, not looking toward her.

"Good night, Dan," she whispered from the doorway. Then she came back to him. "Dan, you won't be sorry?"

"I don't know, Jean," he answered, not whispering.

He stood there listening to her steps on the stairs, her door closing. Then he set the fender closely around the fire, making sure that no coal shot out beyond its bounds, and went up to his own room. Before he closed his door he listened, as he did every night, for any sound from Sue's room.

Down the hall Sue lay awake. She heard Jean's footsteps, very quick and soft on the carpeted stair, the guarded click of her door, then Dan's footsteps, heavier, not so careful. She heard him pause and then close his door with a firm click of the latch. She often heard him come to bed. She knew when he paused that he listened for any sound from her room. Sometimes, she called to him. That little pause was like a caress. But tonight she lay unhappily staring at the dark. She couldn't sleep. The hot milk had had no power to soothe away the bitterness of the evening.

Now in the dark there was something stealthy in the footsteps on the stairs, secret, like their hiding from her the fact that she could never be well, holding out false promises. As if Dan and Jean stole off together to be alone . . . why hadn't they come upstairs together, naturally, talking?

She was frightened at her own thinking. She was absurd to doubt; she had always been secure in Dan's love. But as a young girl she had always been sure that life would be pleasant, good to her, and here she was. a hopeless invalid. Ugly things could happen to her.

She pushed the whole suspicion from her. All she needed to do was to call out and Dan would come running, would take her in his arms and call her foolish; then she thought of him as he was tonight playing bridge, silent, the expression of his face withdrawn. And Jean, why, Jean was her own sister; she was interested in MacLean. There was nothing weak about Dan, and Dan loved her. This suspiciousness was part of being sick. She was always nervous when she didn't sleep. She turned over on her side.

A sound forced its way slowly into her thoughts, a sound of water dripping from the gable onto the balcony outside her window. The snow had begun to melt. The sound was portentous, as though even the universe stirred and changed. Nothing stayed or was secure, not even Dan. But surely Dan.

5

IT was Good Friday. Even in the hospital an atmosphere that belonged neither to a holiday nor to Sunday coated the daily routine with significance. Already pots of Easter lilies had begun arriving; regal clusters on the private floors, single lilies on the wards.

Dan stopped in the staff room on his way out of the hospital. The boys were writing reports on the cases they had seen at the end of the afternoon. A couple of them had already slipped out of their white coats.

Dan had come in in the middle of an ardent discussion. He smiled. It was always the same at this time of year.

In the staff room the subject of next year's plans and appointments was always present behind the talk of this or that case. There was the usual talk of what inexpensive car gave you the most for your money and what plan of life insurance gave you the best protection while you were getting started. Dan knew.

As he left, he heard Tom Barton resuming the discussion; he paused a moment in the hall.

"It's in the spring that the temptation is the strongest to get the hell out of this dump and get going. If we go now, we'll be competent enough to fill the bill of specialist, but we'll be leaving a lot of loose ends just the same."

Change was already in the air. Dan went on down the corridor a little wistfully. His own work here, his own life would go on as it was.

"The boys were hard at it when I dropped in the staff room just now."

Dan had met Stephen Ridley in front of the hospital and they were walking toward the campus together.

"Barton looked as though he were ready to settle the future of medicine, single-handed. I rather envied him; it would be good to be that age again, trying to decide what you were going to do, wouldn't it?"

Stephen didn't answer. Instead he said, "Dan, why don't you go south for a month; take Sue and Agnes Barton along? March is the worst month of the whole year here." He buttoned his coat together as he spoke.

Dan only shrugged.

"I tell you, Dan, you're going to have to do something; you're just going on your nerve. You're stale. What are you doing with that *Maryland Journal* article you promised?"

Dan said nothing. They turned down the diagonal walk. The middle of the walk was dry, but on either side grimy snow still held. Patches of grass showed in front of the old Science building. The forsythia bush that grew close to the steps had a fresh-varnished look. The air was raw and the sky sagged like a wet sheet close to the top of the buildings.

"You know, I kind of resent spring vacation," Stephen remarked. He shouldn't have mentioned the paper. It was getting so you couldn't talk anything but generalities with Dan, he thought. "It always comes in the wrong place for my work and the town has a droop to it with most of the youngsters gone. The ones who stay here working in the library or studying in some empty classroom have a kind of hangdog look."

Dan nodded briefly. "I don't know, it's something to have the diagonal clear." But he glanced around as he said it at the empty steps of the library, the closed look of the Administration office.

"Well, the ivy's starting." Stephen paused on the narrow walk that ran close to the wall of the Science building. The whole side was covered by a ragged mesh of tiny vines overlaid by the gray twistings of the larger branches. At every joining a nubbin of red gleamed like a bead. "Look at that place where the vine's blown down, there's a complete outline left on the wall." He stood looking up at the white lines on the stone, lines as fine as the tracks of sandpipers.

Dan hardly glanced at the vines. He had wanted to talk to Stephen the other night but now he found nothing to talk about. He felt it an effort to listen to Stephen's talk about the vines.

"I wonder how old some of those dead leaves up there are. They get caught in there and the wind can't get them all down. I always notice them in the spring or fall and then in the summer I forget to listen, but I imagine you can hear the old leaves rustle under the new, green crop." Stephen's voice went on in a leisurely, reasonable tone.

Dan grunted. They were reaching the end of the diagonal. He had promised to meet Jean in the library. It was a relief to think of Jean.

"Sue seemed a little upset the last time I saw her," Stephen said abruptly.

Dan glanced at him quickly. "How do you mean? She's more unstable emotionally, I've noticed that; seems to get piqued, almost hurt with Agnes or Jean or myself and then in a couple of hours she's all over it. That isn't like Sue, of course. I keep explaining to Jean that it's only the natural effect of the illness." A look of weariness settled down on his face.

Stephen nodded. "You know we had felt there was

a remission in the disease. But now, I'm not so sure that it isn't advancing."

Out of his anguish of mind, almost without his thoughts motivating his words, Dan said, "It would be a blessing if it were . . ." then he stopped.

"I know," Stephen said, and then as irrelevantly, because they had come to a period, he added in a brighter tone of voice, "I've been wanting to tell you, Dan, you've been doing a wonderful job with your boys. They're as devoted to you as any group I've ever seen. How you've managed it in the midst of this thing I don't know."

"Thanks," Dan said.

Stephen hesitated. He wanted to say something more. Now after he had told Dan how well he'd done with his group was the time to speak out. He would make his tone light to show the contempt he and Stella felt for the idea. He had rehearsed what he would say half a dozen times. He rehearsed it again: People being the rats they are, Dan, they've been quick to say . . . no, think would be a better word . . . you and Jean are seen together so much; even Hutchins mentioned it. . . .

Stephen stared down at the dead grass that had yellowed under the snow and now that the snow had melted lay exposed to the fresh air again. Suspicion and evil-thinking were like that grass. He looked away to the red nubbins on the vines. No faintest whisper of the things people said should cross his lips. Dan might think that he doubted him.

"Well, I promised to pick up Jean at the library so I'll leave you here, Stephen," Dan said.

Dan turned back across the walk, his spirits lightened a little by Stephen's praise. He went up the long flight of shallow steps to the library as eagerly as a student. He tried to check that eagerness.

Since that night after the bridge game, he and Jean had talked only trivialities, exchanged scarcely a glance, and yet, he had the feeling, perhaps Jean had, too, of understanding, of . . . whatever it was, he kept it in his mind as something treasured. It made the days easier. It even made him more patient with Sue. And he had spent more time with Sue; what more could he do?

The large study hall looked almost deserted. He found Jean easily. She was sitting in the meager light from the west windows. He stood outside the door looking at her. A book lay in her lap, but she was not reading. He had gone to meet Jean with Jean in his mind, but with her face in repose Jean's resemblance to Sue was so strong she brought Sue to him more than herself. He pushed the swinging door and at his first step Jean glanced up quickly, smiling, and dispelled the resemblance. She came across to him and they went out of the library together.

"Wait long?" Dan asked.

Jean shook her head. "I've always meant to stop in the library."

"I've spent plenty of time there," Dan said. "Sue used to come over with me evenings."

"It's queer the way I feel as though I knew you and Sue so well just from being in the same places and knowing the same people. When you married Sue, Dan, did I seem like a child to you?"

"Pretty much," he laughed at her. "You were, you know." They reached the end of the diagonal and went through the Engineers' arch out on University Avenue.

They could no more separate Sue from them and be alone together than Dan could stop being himself, Jean thought with a little hopeless settling of her shoulders. As though Dan sensed it, he put his hand through her arm as they walked along past the shop windows.

They went by a bakery and Jean said, "Let's go in and get some hot cross buns to take home."

Standing in the shop, the sweet smell of raisins and sugar frosting on fresh bread came to Jean sharply. It would always be mixed in her mind with the memory of Dan standing by her quietly at the counter. Dan jingled coins in his hand and exchanged them for the paper sack. Then they came out again into the raw air.

"The car's over by the hospital," Dan said.

Would they go on like this all the way, saying nothing that mattered? Jean felt herself straining to know what was in Dan's mind. Now! Jean looked down the street, waiting for Dan to say something about themselves, but they walked the block in silence: Dan's arm still in hers, he swung the silly paper bag in his other hand. She couldn't go on like this. She burst out impetuously,

"Dan, didn't it mean anything to you, the other night?"

Dan's hand tightened on her arm. She looked up at him quickly and was startled out of herself by the sternness of his expression. He looked older and so tired.

"Dan, I'm sorry, shall we go home and have tea with Sue?" she asked gently. Dan nodded.

"Jean, there isn't anything to do but to go on as we are while Sue lives; we mustn't think about ourselves."

"We can't help but think about ourselves, Dan," Jean burst out. "You know we can't. Why can't we recognize that we love each other? That isn't wrong, Dan, and what if it is?" The dreary coldness of the day made her suddenly desperate. "I love Sue, too. This sickness of hers is a horrible, ghastly thing, but we can't let it ruin our lives, too. Perhaps we'd have loved each other anyway, even if Sue hadn't been sick; that would have been worse."

Dan wondered. But his life would have gone on so smoothly Jean would never have come to mean so much. Everything was changed by Sue's illness. He was changed.

"Dan, I've been meaning to mention it to you, but hating to at the same time."

"What, Jean?"

"About Sue. She seems almost, well, almost out of her mind sometimes lately. She looks at me some days in such a way I'm almost afraid. I think she hates me for being well. I mean . . ." Jean faltered . . . "is that all part of the disease or do you think she is losing her . . . her mind?"

Jean watched the two students at the end of the street. Dan was quiet so long she glanced up at him. His face was given to lines. The promontory of forehead and cheekbones and jaw always stood out boldly. It seemed to her that she loved every plane and hollow.

"I don't know, Jean. I've seen her stare at me and wondered, too. I feel as though," he spoke very slowly, "I never had known anything. What I do know does her no good."

He loves her, Jean told herself. He can hardly bear to think of her breaking up. He'll never love me so much.

"It seems to me now sometimes as though I had never known Sue," Dan said. "I try to keep in my mind the way she was. You know, Jean, how she used to see through any kind of pomposity, how quick she was and happy most of the time. But there's nothing left of that Sue."

"Nothing left of that Sue," Dan had said. Jean glanced in the window of the grocery store they passed.

She was free then to love Dan. The damp cold of the day no longer mattered. It could no longer touch her, she carried such warmth of her own in her mind.

Dan opened the door of the car for her.

"I'm starved, Dan, let's eat a bun now. 'Hot cross buns, one a-penny, two a-penny, hot cross buns,' " she chanted, gamin-wise. Dan smiled.

Jean felt suddenly generous. "I forgot I promised to take Donna downtown before dinner," she fabricated quickly. "You and Sue have tea together."

6

YOU look lovely!" Jean stopped in Sue's room after Sue was dressed for the morning. "I do like your hair short, it's so becoming, and you're looking so much better."

Sue looked at Jean, watching her while she said each word, trying to see through her. She gave no sign that she had heard Jean. She did not smile. She only stared.

Jean's voice softened. "Aren't you feeling as well, Sis?" She came swiftly over to the bed and touched Sue's arm.

Sue pulled back from her. "I'm all right," she told her.

Jean looked troubled. She started to speak and thought better of it.

If she could only talk without letting her words slur

and drag she would pour out all her hate. Jean, who was her own sister, with whom she had shared her home. Sue's eyes filled with tears. Her fingers clutched the edge of the blanket. She was trembling. Her face felt hot and dry.

"Go on. Go on downstairs," she told Jean. Let her think what she wanted.

Jean hesitated by the bed, then she went. She would send Agnes up to her.

When she had gone Sue wrenched the blanket between her fists. She opened her mouth in a soundless cry. She rolled her head from one side to the other in the helplessness of her hate. If she stopped hating them for one moment, if she thought about Dan, Dan as he used to be, she would have nothing left. She couldn't stand it. Dan and Jean loved each other. They were nothing to her any longer; she didn't care, she only hated them.

Why was she sure? She knew nothing, really, she tried to tell herself. But she did know; just little things. She had heard Jean call Dan for breakfast. Her voice had sounded different, happier. "Bring Donna, will you, Dan?" Jean had called this morning. Dan had carried Donna downstairs and they had all laughed and she had heard them. She had known how they must be looking across the table at each other.

MacLean hadn't been here for a long time. Dan looked up eagerly when Jean came into the room. Once in a while, he took pains not to look at Jean. She knew; she had watched them.

Her hands loosed the blanket and clutched at the folds of silk at her breast. Jean had given her this and all the time, all the time . . . Sue grabbed the pale green stuff in both hands and wrenched at it. It was hard to tear. She bit it with her teeth and the silk against her teeth made her shudder. Once she was started she tore it across the sleeves and down the back. She tugged it from under her and threw it on the floor in a heap.

They would think her crazy. They might even put her away. Let them; this was no life!

Agnes came with her morning bouillon. Her silence angered Sue. Jean had probably told Agnes she was difficult this morning. She said that about Donna when she was naughty. Sue shook her head when Agnes offered her the bouillon. She closed her eyes and lay still. Agnes was seeing her like this! She would write it down on the chart. There was no privacy now that she was sick. Everything was written down.

Sue knew when Agnes picked up the torn negligee. She heard her pull the cord on the blinds. She felt Agnes' fingers on her wrist.

"You'll have just time to sleep a little before lunch, Mrs. Norton." Agnes was sitting down now, over by the table. Sue was ashamed to open her eyes and look at Agnes. She didn't want Dan and Jean to know about the negligee. They mustn't really think that she was insane. She wasn't, or was this the way insanity began? She had never done anything like this before.

Once, as a child she had hung over the end of an open wagon to see the road roll by under the wheels. She had leaned out so far she had nearly lost her balance and grabbed out wildly to save herself. She had that same feeling now.

Pitifully, like a child, she looked over at Agnes.

"I, the negligee; I wouldn't want Jean . . ." she whimpered.

"I know, Mrs. Norton. I'll see if I can't mend it." She came over to the bed. "Your face is so hot, let me put a cold towel on your head."

The cold was delicious. It spread across her temples up into her hair. Her fingers ached. She let them lie open against the sheet. She made a great effort.

"How is Tom?" she asked.

Agnes laughed. She was pleased. "He's just fine, Mrs. Norton, only he's so wrapped up in some research work he's doing that he keeps forgetting to look for an opening. I guess there's time enough, though. The Whitneys don't know what they're doing next year, either."

But her hate and distrust of them both grew. Only she was crafty now. She didn't give way any more to childish tantrums. She was more co-operative about the light treatment and her extra nourishment. She was waiting.

One of these days, she told herself, she would tell them both that she knew; that she had known for months that she would never get well. Then she would tell them that she knew they loved each other. She would throw it in Dan's face and ask him what his young men who admired him so would think. She thought of phrases that would hurt. "Dr. Norton, whose scientific honesty was so great that he could not accept the Fairchild Medal!" But she would wait a while.

The suspense gave her days new excitement. Agnes told Dr. Norton that Mrs. Norton seemed more interested in things, that she liked to hear about the young people and even called Donna into her room, sometimes, lately.

"Another breathing space," Dan said, steeling himself against new inroads of the disease, but cheered at the same time.

"Aunt Sue, can I have supper up in your room? Jean's going out," Donna said, one afternoon. She stood on one leg in the doorway.

"Of course," Sue said. The child had always been fond of her. It had been Sue's own fault that Donna had dropped off coming. Now her frank curiosity in Sue's speech and the jerking movement of her hands was gone. She took her as a matter of course. Donna lingered in the doorway, watching Sue try to turn the page of a book herself.

"Good for you, Aunt Sue. That was swell!" she burst out naturally.

"Where's Mother going?" Sue asked.

"Oh, Jean and Dan are going into the city to see some opera," Donna explained in disgust. "She has a new dress for it."

"Oh," Sue said. Dan hadn't even mentioned going when he sat talking this noon. They were doing that now, sneaking off together.

Donna went on talking. Sue didn't listen.

"Aunt Sue, you don't like Jean much, do you?" the child asked abruptly.

Sue was startled. She stared at Donna, seeing her face that was so like Jean's. The child eyed her steadily; then she smiled knowingly as though she had found her out.

"Of course, she's your sister, but I mean really?"

Donna was too old for her age, too old to brush aside with a rebuke.

"Really I do, Donna."

Donna twisted a lock of hair. "Sometimes your face gets all funny when you're thinking about her, like just now. But maybe it's because you want to be going to the opera, too."

"Yes, that was it, Donna." She tried to speak more clearly. "Do you love her very much, Donna?" She had not known she was going to ask that question. It came so suddenly to her lips.

"Sure, she's not the mothery kind, but she's the

prettiest of any of 'em; and she lets you alone more. Sure I do."

"She's a dear," Sue said, ashamed of her question.

Sue heard Dan come in a little early. He came straight up to see her. She heard him taking the stairs two at a time. It was because he felt guilty. She hardened her heart. And when he came in she was not beguiled by the sense of strength that came with him nor by the sight of him. She lay back with her head turned toward the window.

"Oh, Dan," she began and made no effort to control the staggering of her voice. "I've been waiting for you. I've felt so queerly all afternoon."

Dan's alarm was genuine. He took her pulse and sat on the edge of her bed watching her anxiously.

"How do you mean, Sue?" he asked gently.

Sue sighed. "Sort of breathless and panicky. When I try to look at something it blurs and that scares me." She closed her eyes. Her eyes *had* blurred a little. She sighed again, wearily.

Dan's hand closed over her own. His hand was so warm and strong. His hands were so like Dan. When he was with her she couldn't remember anything against him. Her hate and doubt seemed unimportant. She brought them back to her: Dan knew she couldn't get well; he was hiding it from her; he and Jean loved each other. Her mind knotted again with hate and suspicion.

Dan brought her one of the familiar little capsules. "This will make you feel better, Sue."

She took the capsule and held it under her tongue. This would make her feel comfortably drowsy but she didn't want that.

"I'll go down and tell Jean I'm home and then I'll be back."

Sue spit the capsule out into her hand and hid it in her pillow case. How obvious Dan was! Jean knew he was here. She must have been waiting for him. Perhaps she whispered to him to go up and see Sue quickly and get it over with so they could go. Dan was talking to Agnes in the hall. Sue strained to hear what they said.

"I think she'll be all right, Dr. Norton. You could call me from the city if that would make you feel better. It seems too bad to have you stay home."

"Well, I'll dress so I'll be ready, but I don't want to go if Sue seems worse," Dan said.

Sue didn't acknowledge to herself what she wanted. It lay, a delicious possibility at the edge of her consciousness. It gave her a secret sense of power. If she let herself acknowledge what she was trying to do she would be ashamed. Even now, a thin tongue of shame licked against her thoughts.

When Agnes came into the room Sue said plaintively, "I don't want Dr. Norton to stay home with me if he has something he intended to do." Now she felt better. She felt noble and self-sacrificing.

When Jean came in in her new dress she said with

instinctive cunning, "Jean, you look pretty enough to be going to the opera." She couldn't be sure whether Jean flushed. She had spoiled their enjoyment now if they did go.

Some part of her mind stood aside in shocked amazement. Where would her hate end? It was destructive, carrying them all with it. Let it! She was stronger than they were, after all. They would see! She would punish them. She pulled herself up straighter against the back of the bed. Her hands knotted together as painfully as her mind.

The phone rang and Agnes told Dan that Dr. Hutchins was on the phone. Dan closed his door to answer, but she could guess. They were going with the Hutchins. Hutch had phoned to say they were starting. It was time if they had dinner in town. Or perhaps they meant to have just a bite and have dinner afterwards. Yes, that would be it, at some night club. They would go there after the opera. The sound of the singing would linger in their ears, making every least thing they did glamorous; going out of the opera house with the crowds of people, driving in the city looking at the store windows, prolonging the evening with dinner, driving back to Woodstock, silently, each person thinking of the opera again.

She wondered what opera they would be going to see. But she wouldn't ask. Later, when they had gone, she would ask to see the paper. It would be in there.

But would they go? It was six-thirty. They would have to hurry.

"Feeling better, Sue?" How becoming the stiff white shirt and the black satin lapels of his coat were! She could see him again giving the Fairchild lecture.

"Do you, dear?" His voice was hopeful.

She felt quite well, but she couldn't stop now. She leaned limply against the pillows. Her voice was weak. "You and Jean are going somewhere, don't stop for me, I'm enough of a drag, now."

"It was nothing, dear, only a very dull evening going into town. I'm glad of an excuse not to go. I just explained to Hutchins," Dan said quickly.

Dan calling the opera dull! There was no truth in any of them any more, not in her, not in Dan or Jean.

"I wish I were dead and out of your way, Dan." Underneath her cunning there was truth in her words. She was ashamed now.

Dan stopped her lips with his hand. He held her face between his warm hands. For an instant she was sure he didn't care whether he went or not. Dan loved her. She had been all wrong. She burrowed her face into his hands until she could touch them with her lips. Jerkily she laid her hands over his and pressed them closer.

"Hurry, Dan, and go. You were all ready to go."

"No, dear, I'm not going now. I'm going to sit here with you."

"Dan, please, I don't want you to stay!" She shook

her head. He mustn't stay. She had built up something on an impulse. She was sorry now. Why had she done it? She hadn't really meant to keep him home. Dan loved opera. "Please, Dan!"

"The Hutchins will stop by for Jean. I'd rather stay with you, dear," Dan said, sensing her agitation, seeing the tears in her eyes.

It was her mind; she hadn't meant to do this. Her mind was no longer a clear, ordered place. It was cluttered and confused. A car came along the driveway outside the window. Dan went downstairs. She heard him call good-by from the porch. She covered her face with her hands.

She heard Agnes outside her door.

"I'm so sorry, Dr. Norton; it seems a shame for you to stay home when you've planned it so long."

"That's all right. I insisted on Mrs. Keller's going. There was no reason for both of us to stay home. I'll be here if you care to go out, Agnes," Dan said.

He read aloud. Sue lay quietly. When she would tell him that it was only because she wanted him near her so much his words to Agnes came up in her mind. "Both of us" Dan had said. She turned her face toward the other side of the room.

Dan put down the book. "That doesn't take hold tonight."

He was thinking about the opera and being with Jean, she told herself. She opened her lips to speak.

They would have it out tonight. She would tell him why she pretended to be sick, why she hated him. But Dan spoke.

"Sue?" His voice sounded different from his reading voice. Perversely she did not answer. She held her eyes closed. Let him beg her to listen. She made her breathing heavier. He reached up and snapped off the light. She heard the flat sound of the book laid against the table. He was going downstairs now, to wait for Jean. All she needed to do was to speak.

"Wait, Dan," was all she needed to say.

He was past the bed now.

When he had gone she wished she had spoken. She lay awake long after she heard Jean come home and the Hutchins drive away, and Dan's door close; until the house was swallowed up in silence and in hate.

7

AGNES stood in the window by Sue's couch. Down in the garden Jean was cutting tulips. Once she paused and waved her shears and the tulips at Sue's window. All the bright colors of the spring morning seemed caught in her hand, snipped off carelessly by her shears. Dan drove through the yard with Donna on the seat beside him and Jean waved to them and called out some greeting that made them laugh.

Agnes turned away from the window and saw Sue's

face distorted in a stiff grimace that she had never seen before. The knuckles of one hand were scrunched against her mouth. Her eyes were closed.

"Why, Mrs. Norton, what is the matter?"

"Nothing." Sue moved her hand down jerkily from her mouth. Her face smoothed into its usual mask.

"Hello, Sue." Jean came in carrying her tulips in a low white bowl. "Only four out yet; I thought you should have the first ones." Brightness came with her. "Look at this one, isn't it lovely?" She cupped her fingers around a delicate pink bloom and her fingertips took on the perfect delicacy of the tulip's curve.

Sue looked at her without glancing at the tulips. She made no answer. Her very stillness moved Jean to chatter.

"It looked so springlike we ate breakfast on the porch this morning and nearly froze. Dan was so tried with me." Laughter filtered through her words. "But Donna was so cold she ate her cereal without any fuss. Sleep well?"

Sue turned her face closer to the pillow. Jean looked questioningly at Agnes.

"I'm afraid Mrs. Norton was awake early," Agnes said, her voice soothing.

"Well, I've got to get dressed and run downtown to the country market. Dan wants some home-made cottage cheese with fresh chives in it he said this morning. What do you crave, Sue?"

Sue spoke slowly. "To get well . . . or else be dead." The words sounded dully in the room. They dragged a heavier silence after them. They made the four tulips look foolishly garish. They drained the animation from Jean's face. They brought Agnes to Sue's side.

"You're going to feel so much better now with warm weather, Mrs. Norton. If you would just try it again I'm sure you could walk a little."

"Sue, don't talk that way," Jean pleaded. She hesitated a second and then went out and closed the door quietly behind her.

All through her bath Sue was silent and Agnes did not talk.

When she was left alone, Sue's face became distorted again. She raised her knuckles to her mouth and bit them until the teeth left a mark on the skin. Tears ran down her face and she wiped them off awkwardly with her sleeve. Then she turned her face into the pillow and cried so that her whole body was shaken with the crying and she fell to coughing.

The way they waved to each other! And Jean's coming upstairs to bring her the tulips guiltily because that was all that was left for her. It was more than she could stand. She and Dan had loved each other for almost twenty years, but it couldn't have been love, really, only something thin and unsubstantial. Or could love stand death and separation, but not disease?

When Dan left for the war there had been no love

like theirs. He had written her on a page torn from a prescription blank: "It was like leaving part of myself there on the platform. I am only half a person without you." She had the piece of paper still.

And when he came back, their life had never flatted. Everything they had done, they had shared. She had always known what Dan was working for. When he was discouraged about a case she had always known, even before he told her about it, and when things went well they had had such celebrations! Other husbands and wives had their worries over their children's illnesses, but she had shared as deeply Dan's worries over patients whose names she did not even know.

How could Dan change like this?

Agnes came in with an eggnog and a capsule. When she hadn't slept in the night they gave her one of these. She wouldn't wake up now till afternoon. She took the capsule and drank the eggnog. Better to be all body and no mind. She didn't have the strength now to think any more.

The house was very still, with a quietness that seemed to share some property in common with the mild afternoon light. Sue always wakened this way and lay testing out the time. It had grown warmer; one of the tulips had opened wide to show the purple marking around the stamens. She felt refreshed and hungry.

Suddenly, absurdly, she knew what she craved. She didn't want to have lunch brought her on a tray, carefully, daintily prepared. She wanted to go out to the icebox herself and *see* what she wanted. She would like to take a paring knife, the little brown-handled one that had been in the kitchen drawer ever since she began keeping house, and cut herself crispy bits from a cold roast, there where all the sweetness of the juices was basted into it.

She could almost taste the meat. She would keep on carving slivers from the roast until she had made disgraceful inroads into it. Perhaps she would have a glass of milk, too. She was hungry as she hadn't been in a long time. She reached out for the small silver bell on her table. Her hand was too clumsy. She knocked the bell off on the floor.

Agnes came in smiling. "Hungry? It's almost four."

"Yes." She was coming to answer more and more briefly.

"Dr. Norton came in and sat here about half an hour this noon, waiting to see if you'd wake up. He dropped off to sleep, himself."

Dan had been here, sitting by her. She was pleased. Then she remembered.

Her mind that had been so clear and serene and coated with pleasure when she woke, clouded. Dan only pretended to love her. Perhaps he even wished she would die. She felt tired as though she had not slept at all. When Agnes brought her lunch she was not hungry.

Agnes took the tray. "You must eat a good dinner tonight to make up for such a light lunch; you'll be on your feet sooner if you keep up your strength. Would you like to hear the Saturday afternoon concert, Mrs. Norton? It should be on now."

Sue nodded, not caring. Her mouth twitched with anger. They were all in a conspiracy against her. They all treated her as though she were a child, telling her lies.

But she could not listen to the music. A long time ago, when she had felt secure she had loved music; when Dan loved her and she had thought she would get well. Now her mind had no stillness in which to listen.

When the doorbell rang, the radio sputtered as though some string on one of the violins had broken. Agnes answered the door and came back to tell her that Peter Whitney was downstairs to see Dr. Norton.

"Tell him to come up here until Dr. Norton comes," Sue said. It was so dull lying here; it would be good to see someone else. She hadn't seen anyone outside this house since that night they had played bridge with MacLean. She had had no desire to see anyone, her mind had been so full of hate. She had used to like to see the medical students and interns and instructors, to guess what kind of doctors they would make.

"How do you do, Mrs. Norton," Peter said. "I'm sorry to bother Dan, but I've had an opening up the state offered me; I wanted to ask him what he thought of it. If there is any chance of an opening here, of course . . ." he laughed.

Sue had a malicious desire to damage Dan for this young man. This was the one Dan thought so promising. He adored Dan, no doubt. Let him know that Dan was not so perfect, that he could love someone else when his wife was dragging out a miserable existence.

"How splendid!" Agnes said to Peter. "You're lucky; Tom's praying for one."

Peter was like so many young men who had come to see Dan. They were all alike, so young, so confident, and they all came to Dan.

"I thought Tom wanted to stay on here," Peter said.

Agnes flushed. "No, he wants to get started in practice; he wants me to stop nursing. Does your opening sound pretty good?"

"It depends on the man who wants an associate. He was in Dan's class here. His name is Nelson, Arthur Nelson in South Haven."

They were so full of plans, Dan's young men; and their wives were always with them at this stage, Sue thought.

Peter took out his pipe. "Now that it's spring we're all getting worked up over next year. If we could just work away and not bother about the wise thing to do next . . ." he laughed. "Can you remember when Dan was at this stage, Mrs. Norton, or didn't he ever worry you about plans?"

"Yes," Sue said. "Dan almost went to a town in New

England to practice, but he liked the teaching so much."

"I do, too," Peter said ruefully. He rubbed his hand back over his shock of hair and Sue noticed how shiny his coat-sleeve was. "But you have to live, don't you?" he looked at Agnes.

"I should say," Agnes nodded. "There's Dr. Norton, now."

Oh, yes, she could remember. She remembered how they used to plan the future. "When I'm a professor, Sue," Dan used to say, "you shall have a sable coat." And she had laughed at the absurdity of wanting a sable coat.

Now that she was started, she kept on remembering; the time they had invited Professor Carlyle and his wife to dinner and the steak was burned; the only time Dan had been sick and she had sat up in the bathroom reading *Osler's Practice of Medicine* to figure out for herself what he had. And Dan had come in to find her there and laughed so hard she knew he must be better.

There was the time Dan tried for the research assistantship in Neurology and Rob Goddard was appointed. Dan had tried to act as though he didn't care but the disappointment rankled a long time. Dan usually succeeded. For every case he couldn't cure there were ten that he sent away better. He didn't dwell on those hopeless ones; he couldn't, of course, or he wouldn't be able to stand it.

Like a key turning in the lock, the words "every case he couldn't cure" opened a door in her mind. She was just such a case. Every day he came home to be confronted by his failure to make her better. It must be hard for him. For the first time since the early thaw she realized that she was thinking of Dan without thinking of herself.

Something in Peter's eagerness reminded her of Dan as he had been the year they came to Woodstock. She sent Agnes to dig out a leather case in a trunk in the attic, feeling bitterly that she was not even able to rummage for her own keepsakes.

When Agnes came back with the case, Sue set it up on the table by the bed. The picture of Dan was dated by the stiff collar, the different cut to the coat lapels, his boyish look. It startled her to see how much older he had grown. She wasn't aware of it living with him day after day.

It the same case was a picture of herself. It was even more perfectly dated by the fancy shirtwaist and the way her hair was combed. The alert look of her own face comforted her. How unaware they looked, she and Dan, that life could change them, how far removed from illness she seemed, and Dan from care or worry.

Sue was still looking at the pictures when Dan came up from talking with Peter.

"Hello, dear, what have you there?"

Sue didn't answer and he came over and took her hand and picked up the picture of her.

"I always liked this one of you," he said easily, watching his words so that they wouldn't betray how sharply the difference between then and now struck him. How much expression her face had then! He put the picture on the table and looked at the one of himself. That was safer, but it irked him to come suddenly on it.

"What a head of hair I had then," he laughed. "I look like a pretty cocky fellow there."

"You've changed," Sue said slowly. "I never thought you would change so much."

He could never be sure, lately, just what Sue meant; her whole manner and way of saying things had become so different.

"Well, we all change," he said lightly, putting the pictures over on the mantel, but his brain mocked at the bromide and sickened at the change in Sue's features from those in the picture. He moved a chair over by her and sat down. He started to take her pulse but she jerked her wrist away from him.

"What's the use, Dan?" she spoke almost roughly. This was one of her bad days, he thought wearily.

"All right, dear, you're bothered enough," he said gently and touched her hand with his lips instead. Quick tears filled her eyes.

"Dan, Jean's home, and she says do you want her to leave the car out?" Donna ran into the room. "H'lo, Aunt Sue," she added carelessly.

"Yes, tell her to leave the car and you run along,

Donna," Dan said, but his spirits quickened. There was no sentimentality, no heaviness or moods about Jean. After a few moments Dan went on downstairs.

Sue heard him speak to Jean in the hall. For a sickening second she wanted to call out to them; to tell them now that she knew they loved each other. She had an appetite for dramatic things these days, a terrible urge to startle people. They passed her over as Donna did; she was sick so she didn't matter. But they would have to reckon with her. She would make them so ashamed they would never get over it.

Her mouth sucked in at one corner until the lips were crooked. Her nostrils dilated, leaving white spots at either side of the nose. She lifted her head back defiantly and the line of her throat bulged. She caught sight of her own image in the mirror, but it was so ugly, so unlike her as she seemed to herself that she looked away quickly. Her eyes fell on the two little pictures that Dan had set on the mantel.

That girl was herself. She used to be pretty. And Dan's picture! How young he looked! The two pictures took on an identity apart from the persons she and Dan were now. The people in the pictures knew nothing about disappointment or tragedy. Her eyes watered foolishly for their very youth and sureness. She felt about them as she might have if they were her children. She knew so much more than they did; she knew how things would turn out for them. It was a pity!

Dan's strength wasn't great, after all. He was weak.

And she had grown into a suspicious, bitter old woman.

But why shouldn't she? If Dan was untrue, even in spirit, there was nothing left in life for her. Dan was far away from her. Even when he sat reading to her here he was separated from her by the length of the upstairs hall. She could get no farther than the little table that held the night-lamp. She could only see the glass knob of Dan's door catching the light. When Dan did come to her he pitied her. Her sprawling body, sprawling as it had that early morning, revolted him.

She didn't want to see the images of themselves any more. It was better not to go back or remember anything, not to care very much for anybody else.

But the pictures drew her eyes to them. She had been so proud of Dan then, of herself. You had to have something to be proud of in yourself, even when you were sick, or you were lost. Dan couldn't be proud of turning away from her to Jean. For his own sake, Dan mustn't . . . change.

She looked across to the tulips bright now in the bar of late afternoon sun that lay across them. She realized suddenly that she had gone over the heavy knowledge she had fought ever since that night the snow melted in the early thaw . . . and she had not burst into tears this time! One thing was as true as the pale green blades of the tulip leaves; she could never hate Dan. Whatever he might do. She might have known that. A kind of joy ran through her.

Then the elation left her. "Oh, God!" she whispered

into the pillow, pounding it with her jerking fists, letting the weak tears run out of her eyes onto the pillow case. "He mustn't change. He must love me."

She must not cry. She had started the day with crying and Dan would be upset if he found her crying.

8

PETER drove straight home from his talk with Dan. He knew Elsa would be waiting to hear what Dan thought of the opening. Dan had been as interested as though he, himself, were going out to look the proposition over. But that was the way with Dan.

One thing he had said Peter did not tell Elsa, but it stayed in his mind. It seemed to him that Dan had been thinking of himself. "If you've stayed on in a place like this, you have just as many doubts about the wisdom of your decision as if you'd gone out into practice. The things that are coming to you seem to find you out wherever you are . . ." Peter knew he was thinking of Mrs. Norton's illness . . . "and the good things, too, Peter. If you're going to do any original clinical work you can do it just as well in South Haven, if you have any resourcefulness."

The next day, Peter and Elsa drove up the state to South Haven.

"We'll make a holiday of the trip, Elsa, whatever it turns out to be." Peter had bought a spring chicken to fry for their lunch.

"I call that extravagant!" Elsa had scolded, eyeing the bill.

"Hush, woman! Who knows, this day's decision may be the turning-point of our career," Peter had announced dramatically. "We'll offer up a young cock to Aesculapius at 42 cents a pound!"

They left the baby with Mrs. Janowski and drove over to the Nortons' to get the letter Dan had promised.

"This is fun in the middle of an ordinary week, Peter."

Peter grinned. "I hope they have one hell of a day in the out-patient. I hope Watkins perspires and rides the boys and everybody gets on edge!" He let out a long whistle. "What a day, Els!"

When they rang the Nortons' doorbell Donna came running around the side of the house. "My, you're early; Jean and Dan are still eating breakfast."

They followed her through the house that was dark and too warm after the bright coolness of the April morning.

"Are you going on a picnic?" Donna turned to ask.

"Yes, sort of a picnic," Elsa laughed.

Through the window they could see Jean and Dan at the small table set in the sun beyond the porch steps.

They sat so quietly, not eating, not seeming to move; as quiet as a picture. In spite of the sun on Jean and the sparkle of silver and glass, Elsa felt a certain sadness about them.

"See, there they are; Jean loves eating outdoors. She says she likes feeling the cold on her ankles and the sun on her neck," Donna told them as though Jean were the child and she the adult.

When they opened the screen door of the porch and stepped outside, Dan waved to them. "Come and have some coffee with us before you start off."

"And a popover," Jean added. "You'll have a glorious ride today, won't you?" She sent Donna for cups and hot popovers.

"Don't be in a hurry about South Haven, Peter. Take time to think it over if you don't feel sure. There are plenty of other places, you know."

"And you're really thinking of practicing there!" Jean exclaimed. Elsa resented Jean's tone that was so casual, so indifferent to this thing that mattered so much to them.

"We're going up to look it over, anyway," Peter said.

"How exciting!" Jean said pleasantly, but in her mind she felt a sense of injustice. Peter and Elsa had no problems; they had each other, all they had to do was to find a place to live. "I'm sure Sue is awake. Do run up and say good morning to her, Elsa." It had come to be a habit to think of anything that might interest Sue, though, sometimes, Sue seemed only irritated.

Elsa went up to Sue's room. She remembered that first evening in this house when she had found Mrs. Norton. Now on this spring morning, just as they were starting to South Haven, Mrs. Norton's illness seemed even more tragic. Distaste rose in her mind. She would be quick about it.

Mrs. Norton was alone.

"Good morning. We're going off to try our luck and I ran up to ask you to pray for us." Elsa's smile was very bright. She felt herself talking too rapidly, trying not to notice Mrs. Norton's jerking movements, trying to talk directly to her eyes.

"Peter told me about it," Sue said.

"We're taking a fried chicken for lunch and I'm wearing my best hat," Elsa chattered. She caught sight of herself in the mirror across the room; all her thoughts came back to herself. "May I powder my nose here? I was so busy getting the baby ready for the day that I got disheveled."

Sue smiled.

Elsa powdered her nose, straightened her hat and touched her lips with a lip-stick.

"Now I feel ready to fight for the place if Peter wants it!" She turned from the mirror, slipping the cap of the lip-stick back on. The pop as it slid into place was loud.

"May I do you?" Elsa asked impulsively, wanting to say something foolish and amusing.

"Why, yes." Sue gave a little laugh of pleasure.

Elsa was very gentle. She held Sue's chin in one hand. The color looked too bright against the paleness of her skin.

"It's very becoming, Mrs. Norton."

Sue looked at herself across the room. She liked the tighter feeling of the skin of her lips. The firm streak of color did give more definiteness to her features.

"There's nothing like lip-stick to set you up," Elsa said. "I must run. Peter wants to get started I know." Elsa came over and kissed her quickly on the cheek.

Sue could hear her running down the stairs. She heard Dan and Jean call out to them and the slam of a car door; then the car driving away down the road.

Jean and Dan went around to the driveway to watch them go off.

"I feel paternal," Dan said. "Whitney's the best of the group. Keith's more brilliant, but he's not quite found himself yet. . . ." Dan seemed to lose himself thinking about them.

How could he be so absorbed, Jean wondered. These young doctors and their wives would go away to their own lives and she and Dan would be left just as they had been for months, condemned to live on in this house, separated from each other by Sue. She and Dan were caught in a trap; no, it wasn't a trap, call it something more polite; say it was a dance; she and Dan the center figures, standing still, posing, striking attitudes while the others danced, but they were caught as surely as in a trap. She watched the Whitneys' car turn off onto University Avenue.

"Well, I must get over to the hospital," Dan said.

Jean went on into the house, feeling herself shut in with sickness. She went up to see Sue. She could tell her about the Whitneys going. Things to talk about with Sue were hard to find some days.

A half shadow lay over Peter and Elsa as they drove out University Avenue past the fraternity houses and the elms, newly touched with green, and the frieze of students along the walks.

"Mrs. Norton's sickness seems to tinge that whole house, in a way, doesn't it?" Elsa said. "Oh, Peter, she's so pathetic. I put lip-stick on and, trying to be humorous, I asked her if I could do her lips and she wanted me to. Peter, imagine Mrs. Norton with lip-stick!" Peter shook his head.

But the day was theirs. They drove out from under that shadow into the sun. Tulips craned long green necks to see beyond their neat plots. The yellow flame of the forsythia bushes burned riotously on professorial lawns. The sibilant sound of roller-skates rose above the noise of passing cars. On the lawn of some fraternity house, two lanky youths played catch and the satisfying ping of the ball biting into the leather mitt was another sound and sign of the spring morning in Woodstock.

"It seems more than nine months ago that we came here, doesn't it, Els?"

"Twice that long, so much has happened," Elsa answered and wondered what really had happened. They had moved into a house, they were part of a group, they knew the Nortons, the baby was walking; nothing had happened, after all.

They passed through a small town: a store, a gasoline station and an automobile repair shop, two churches and a school. A sign on a picket fence read "H. B. Conklin, M.D." Elsa looked eagerly at the shabby white house back of the fence. There was a side door with the words "Walk In" clearly printed above the mail slot.

"Peter, there's a doctor's sign. Do you suppose he ever makes a living?"

"Sure; living wouldn't be high here. He probably has patients scattered all over the country."

"The house didn't look as though he were prosperous," Elsa said. "Not that it matters too much," she added quickly, "only it looks run down, sort of defeated."

"I suppose that's up to the doctor," Peter answered soberly. "If I could get someone in my neighborhood to have quintuplets now and then, I'd do well enough. Or I might persuade my wife to have them!"

"Silly!"

They had left the doctor's house a mile or so behind them when Peter said, "I presume he came from Woodstock once."

"Who?"

"The doctor from that town we passed."

"Oh. It makes our going out like this to find a niche a little . . . prosaic, doesn't it?" Elsa said.

"Well, I suppose it is, really," Peter answered slowly.

"Oh, Peter, you're so ready to take life as it comes," Elsa said, half irked.

"No, I'm not. I don't think I'm the only doctor who ever went out to practice, if that's what you mean."

Elsa didn't answer. Peter stripped the thing down so; she wanted him to be tremendous, to aim at the moon. He was too reasonable.

"Let's eat lunch before we get there, Peter. Once we're there, we'll know what it's like. Maybe we'll be disappointed; let's put it off a little."

Peter laughed at her, but he, too, felt an irrational reluctance to be there now that they were so near. When they were ten miles outside of the town the signs began: "South Haven Hardware," "The Golden Calf Café" . . .

"That was a poetic flight!" Peter said.

"Everybody shops at Emory's!" Elsa read each sign aloud. If they came to live here these signs would come to have a personal meaning. Perhaps Peter would take care of the man who owned Emory's. Peter would say, "Old Mr. Emory who has rheumatism."

The road fell slightly and they saw the lake ahead of them through a thin lattice of birch trees. At this lower end of the lake there was a cluster of cottages, still closed for the winter, looking damp and bedraggled. The air of brightness they achieved in summer by means of a strip of awning, a deck chair, curtains at the window was lacking now.

"Do you suppose all the people of South Haven come out here for their summers?"

Peter shook his head. "We won't, that's a cinch. But the lake isn't to be sniffed at."

"No, it's lovely here." They were both anxious to be pleased with this country if it was to be theirs.

They ate their lunch along the lake, but they took less time about it than they had meant. Peter had spread out the car robe and thrown himself down upon it, but there was no relaxation in his mind. Elsa was careful not to get crumbs on her dark blue suit. Their talk was still fragmentary; surface comments about the lake, what they could do in summer if they should live here.

"Put a sailing canoe on this lake . . ." Peter began, forgetting to finish his sentence. He was wondering what kind of hospital facilities the town had. His face was serious. Elsa scarcely noticed that Peter had left his sentence unfinished. A deep excitement underlay their thoughts. After all, they might live their whole lives in this town. The chicken Elsa had fried that morning might as well have been bread and cheese.

"Well, Els, let's go see," Peter said and a smile broke up the seriousness of his face.

They washed their hands in the lake water that was so cold now in the spring. Elsa saw a pebble along the edge that was sharply marked with black and white and washed thin as a piece of cardboard. She picked it up and polished it with her handkerchief. "Here, Peter, for good luck." She slipped it in his pocket.

It was ten o'clock that night before they started back.

"Whew! Well, that's settled. Kind of a strain, but not so bad as I expected."

"The Nelsons are rather nice," Elsa murmured inadequately. Then she waited. Was Peter elated? Was it really a good opening?

"Dr. Nelson's a sound fellow, I think. He was very generous about arrangements. I don't think I'll have any trouble building up a good practice there. While I was waiting he asked me to see a case. She looked like a neurotic, all right; sounded like it, too, but that's just the kind Dan says you slip up on. At first, I didn't find anything and then . . ."

Elsa wasn't listening. How maddening Peter was! With all there was to talk over he was more excited about a case than the opening. Didn't he sense what a cold feeling of flatness the evening had left her with? The future stretched ahead prescribed, all laid out. Maybe they had decided too fast.

"What's the matter, Els; didn't you like it?"

"Yes," Elsa answered slowly. "I suppose we're lucky."

"Mrs. Nelson's pretty stereotyped, isn't she?"

"Oh, she's not bad," Elsa admitted grudgingly. " 'Our boy is at Harvard now. He's a fine, big fellow, an inch taller than his Dad; I suppose he'll go into medicine, too,' " she mimicked Mrs. Nelson's voice and manner. Then she could stand it no longer. "Peter, I looked at the Nelsons and I could just see us twenty years from now. Oh, they're successful enough; that's the trouble. I can't put my finger on it, but I feel that I don't want to be like them. They don't seem to have any . . ." she shrugged her shoulders hopelessly.

"I know, Els, but, of course, we don't know the Nelsons; they may have started out feeling the way we do."

"Then that makes it all the worse. It's exactly what Dan said was apt to happen to all of us when we left Woodstock."

"I know what you mean. I had that feeling when I first went into the Medical Arts Building. Then Nelson asked me to see this patient and when I was through I'd forgotten everything else and I felt that the work was the whole thing. There's material enough there for me to make a name for myself if I've got it in me."

Elsa was silent. Peter changed the subject, but it lay heavily in both their minds. When they reached the place where they had stopped for lunch Peter drove to the side of the road.

"Let's get out and get some air."

They sat on the running-board of the car, shielded from the wind.

"See the Dipper up there?" Peter asked as though it were just any night.

Elsa felt a rush of gratitude toward Peter. She looked up at the sky. The night had a spacious quality. There was room to live their lives the way they had meant. There was no loneliness; they would always be together in the things they wanted out of life. Absurdly, Elsa felt reassured. The doubts of the day disappeared with Peter beside her. He put a kind of bravery into her. All that anyone ever had, all that mattered was theirs.

"Oh, Peter, was anybody ever so silly, so full of doubts?"

"I love you for being silly."

"We've got to go; we won't be back before morning as it is!"

"Who cares?"

They laughed. The laughter echoed strangely on the lake. The headlights of their old car seemed brighter than the proud aura of the neon lights above the lower end of the lake.

9

ALL day Sue thought about the Whitneys. Now they would be driving into town. At the last minute they would hate to make up their minds. Elsa must be about twenty-three. Sue, herself, had been twenty-two when she and Dan went up on the Boston and Maine to look at the town where Dan's uncle was in practice. She had been a little car-sick between the swaying of the train and the excitement. It was so hot. Dan had said, "If you think this is hot you should have been in the trains in France." It was only two years after the war, she remembered. Dear Lord, how much she remembered!

"Jean, do you remember when I wrote that Dan and I might go to Greenfield to practice?" she asked when Jean came in.

"Greenfield? No," Jean said. "Recently?"

"No, when Dan was an instructor. And then we decided to scrimp a little longer and stay here."

"But now it takes more than scrimping along to stay here," Agnes said. "Tell us about it, Mrs. Norton." She must remember to tell Dr. Norton that Mrs. Norton was unusually animated this morning.

"I wanted to go there," Sue said in her queer high voice that never sounded like her own. She wished she had told Elsa about their trip. "But I left it up to Dan." She remembered how pleased Dan was when she said it didn't make any difference to her. It was unthinkable that she had ever set out to hate Dan.

"Sue, your lips! I've been staring at them," Jean said. "You've got lip-stick on!"

"Elsa did them. And I shall get dressed today." She hadn't been dressed since the night of the Fairchild lecture; housecoats, negligees, but not dressed. She hadn't cared whether she was dressed or not.

She saw the protest in Jean's face, Agnes' concerned expression and said, "I think I need my hair waved too."

Jean hesitated. She glanced over at Agnes. "That's fine; I'll call up right now," she promised as though to please a fractious child.

Sue lay still thinking that sometimes just to watch Jean made her feel as though she, herself, were lithe and quick. But when Agnes struggled to get her arms into the dress and her limbs were rigid and jerked unmanageably that feeling left her. It was no wonder that Dan turned away from her to Jean, she told herself bitterly.

But Dan had loved her body. "I could write my own song of Solomon about you, Sue," he had said. He had kissed her shoulders and her breasts and her thighs. " 'Tisn't 'beasty,' Sue," he had whispered. And it wasn't; how well she knew now.

She mustn't do this. She must separate herself from remembering, even though it left her pitifully unprotected. She was stronger when she didn't hug all their old happiness to her. There was a kind of strength in this separateness that the young girl in the picture had known nothing of: that Jean wouldn't understand. It was hard to think of Jean without hate. She was glad when the girl from the college beauty shop came.

The girl's eyes were curious. She tired her. The clamps fitting on her hair pulled. But after she had gone Sue slept a while. Then Agnes helped her over to the couch. She had not tried to walk for so long her legs ached with the effort.

She wore stockings today. The stockings and the lipstick made her feel less like an invalid. If she didn't move, she thought, looking into the mirror, she looked quite normal.

It was already four o'clock. Queer how the day escaped into nothingness. She had done nothing and yet another day had gone. And this same day had been so full for Peter and Elsa! She had no life unless she measured it against someone else's. She wondered what kind of a day it had been for Dan.

She loved Dan more than Jean could. She must make him see that. She must not get so hurt and hide herself away in silence. What if she couldn't live! But she wouldn't use that; that would only make him pity her more. She stared helplessly at herself in the mirror.

The whole room was reflected there like a painting. "Number 81, Woman on a Couch," it might be called in the catalogue. The figure of the woman, the furniture of the room wouldn't matter. It was the light that made the painting. The way the water in the glass on the dresser immediately in front of the mirror caught all the brightness there was in the room and held it. The rest of the room, the cretonne flowers of the couch, the red of the woman's lips, the blue cover of the book on the table were dull beside that water.

Her terrible voice, her face that had no expression, her jerking movements that would only grow more hideous must sink out of focus like the rest of the room. Surely there was something left in her to catch the light.

Now it was five-thirty. Dan might come any minute. The day gathered itself together and took on the property of time. It was no longer amorphous but arranged in packets of seconds, minutes, hours. It no longer lagged. It walked as Jean walked. It even hurried as Elsa had hurried down the stairs.

She had no time now for childish figures. The day grew almost too hurried for endurance. She heard Dan's car on the driveway.

And downstairs, Jean was waiting for Dan.

When he came in she called out to him, making her voice casual even though she wanted to run to him.

"Dinner's ready as soon as you come down."

Evenings fell into a kind of routine, almost a ritual. Dan went first upstairs to see Sue. Not until he came down again could Jean feel he was quite hers. Always they spoke of Sue first when they sat down at the table.

Jean told him how she had seemed, or what she had done. Sue had her meals when they were having theirs. In the pauses that fell easily between them when they sat alone they could hear the fragile clink of dishes as Agnes carried up Sue's tray or even a faint sound from Sue's room.

Donna sat at the piano practicing. The little tinkling notes seemed to measure off Jean's waiting. Donna finished and looked at Jean.

"Good, dear. Would you like to start dinner?" Then Donna would be through before they were. She and Dan could sit together and talk a little about themselves. Dan couldn't tell Donna a Brownie story that went on and on through the length of the meal. She contrived so hard for a few minutes with Dan.

"O.K.," Donna agreed cheerfully. "Shall I go tell Dan dinner's ready?"

"No," Jean said quickly. "No, he's busy with Aunt Sue." She never called him away except with her mind. Then she thought of Sue today. She hadn't seemed to stare at her so. She had had her hair waved and tried to walk across the room. She hadn't wanted to do that since that night she had had the fit of laughing. But she was queer. She talked so little. Her face might as well have been covered by one of those clay facial masks, all but her eyes. Her eyes seemed darker and brighter.

There was Dan!

"I'm sorry, Jean. You should have gone right ahead.

Donna has the right idea; she waits for no one. Donna, you'll make an excellent doctor's wife if you learn to live your own life." Dan liked to talk to Donna in a half serious, half teasing tone of voice. But Dan's joking words fell with neat irony on Jean's mind. She could never live her own life again without Dan.

While Donna was there she talked about the new tulips that were up; the last tea of the season for the "medical wives" . . . she was waiting for Donna to pop the last strawberry in her mouth.

"May I skate until dark, Jean?"

Jean scarcely heard the request before she said, "Yes, dear, run along. Another cup of coffee, Dan?"

Dan handed his cup across the table. He seemed hardly aware of her tonight. She wished they had eaten at a card-table on the porch. Meals in the dining-room must remind him so often of Sue. Jean had never taken her place at the table. She sat where she had the first night she arrived, at Dan's right, Donna across from her. "We'll keep that for Sue," she had said once and Dan had seemed pleased.

"Sue was dressed. Agnes said she tried getting over to the couch by herself. It's been two months or more since she's even talked about trying to walk. I'm going to bring her downstairs for a little," Dan said.

Resentment lined Jean's mind. Sue couldn't get better, yet she held their lives entirely in her hands. She seemed better or worse and Dan was instantly absorbed in her condition. She had moods of melancholy when she seemed half-crazy and the whole house was depressed. Even Donna seemed to catch the atmosphere. After Sue made Agnes take her to the Fairchild lecture she had been worse and then she had improved until the night she burst out laughing at the cocktail party. She had gotten too tired. Any excitement or seeing people exhausted her. Dan seemed curiously blind to that.

"She really seemed brighter tonight." Dan finished his coffee. "She asked how my day went. She hasn't done that in weeks."

Did it mean that he actually hoped? "Maybe she is better, Dan."

He shook his head. His face in the candlelight stood out more lined with weariness. "No, no real improvement, but it's something." Jean sat quietly until Dan pushed back his chair.

"I'll light the fire. If we have the door on the porch open it won't be too warm and it will look good to her," Jean said when they went into the other room.

"She'll like that," Dan said. He laid the afghan on his big chair and moved the stool in front of it.

Jean had thought they might drive after dinner. The house suffocated her. Dan was away all day, out of hearing of that shrill, staggered voice. She had sat with Sue while Agnes went out. She had asked Sue if she could read to her, but Sue had said she wanted to sleep after she had her hair done. When she woke up, she had sat perfectly still staring in the mirror in a queer abstracted way.

Jean stood by the fire watching the flames take hold. She could take Donna to a movie. She could call up MacLean, he would be glad enough to take her driving. If she stayed here all evening and watched Dan worrying over Sue she would go crazy herself. She went out to telephone, but before she called the number Donna came in.

"Have a good time, dear?" Jean asked.

"Fine, I went over to Mary Page's and had ginger ale."

"How was Mrs. Page?"

"Fine. She asked if we were going to live here all the time now?"

"What did you say?" Jean asked sharply.

"I said we were. We are, aren't we, Mummy?" Donna seldom called her Mummy, only when she wanted something very much.

"Yes," Jean said slowly. "I think we are, Donna." She had been right, then; it hadn't been only in her mind. People did gossip about her. They tried to find out about her from Donna! How much did Donna sense of the currents of feeling in the house? Donna looked at her, sometimes, with such a shrewd expression on her face; she was no longer entirely a child.

Jean went upstairs with her arm around Donna's shoulders in a protective gesture. If she could only fill her life with Donna, but she couldn't. She heard Dan and Agnes bringing Sue down the hall.

Sue felt her stiffness as Dan picked her up. Her body held rigid instead of leaning against him. But Dan was strong. The hall was not so long as it had been that morning she fell. It was good to see the downstairs hall from the landing.

"Look good to you?"

She pressed his shoulder rather than trying to answer. She should have tried to come downstairs more often. It had been pride and hate and self-pity more than her weakness that had kept her upstairs.

She caught her breath as Dan carried her into the room and settled her in a chair. For an instant the room was strange. There was only the fire-light. It was not yet dark outdoors. After her four walls the room was so big. The door stood open on the porch. It seemed a simple thing to walk across the sill and the porch outdoors. She felt the coolness and the wide reach of the spring twilight.

Agnes was asking if she were comfortable. Dan poked the fire and sat down across from her.

"Jean's up putting Donna to bed, I guess," Dan said, as though she must wonder where Jean was.

But she was oddly alone in this room; then, slowly, it became hers again. She had chosen the curtains. There was a little mend in the one by the bookcase. Her eyes touched the place. She remembered when they hung the picture over on the west wall. She knew without looking that the big volume of *Don Quixote* would be on the middle shelf. Her eyes found the shelf and the thick gilt and blue back was proof that nothing was changed. Everything was as it had been. She would get well. Dan loved her. How foolish she had been. Her eyes came back to Dan.

"Your eyes move around the room faster than Donna's," Dan said.

"It seems so good to be downstairs again," Sue tried to say. But when her words slid together in that toneless sing-song she heard them with a kind of amazed horror. Afterwards she sat watching the fire not trying to speak.

Agnes went out and she had Dan to herself. This was what she had waited for all day. She wondered if Jean had waited for him, too. She had to force herself to speak again. She hunted for a safe topic, as though she were a hostess with a shy guest.

"When the Whitneys went off I remembered the time we went up to Greenfield."

Dan smiled. Did he remember or did her voice put him off? She tried to ignore her voice.

"You've never been sorry, have you, Dan?"

Dan frowned. "No, I've always liked it here." Sue's mind seemed so clear tonight. Just when he had felt her mind was mercifully dulled . . . perhaps it was only about things in the past that she could think clearly. He hunted for a way to test her out. He picked up the paper.

"Reading about Vienna makes you pretty sick, doesn't it?"

"Yes," she said. Sue was looking in the fire. She seemed to have no interest in the subject. It was only in the past; but he began reading aloud until Jean came in.

Why had he changed the subject so quickly? Dan couldn't stand thinking back to those days because unfaithfulness or a shadow of turning would have been unthinkable then. Vienna, what was Vienna but any human being forced to live life on different terms, in fear of death, without hope. China, Spain, Sue Norton . . . a million human beings or one, it all came down to the same meaning in the end.

"Sue, it's great to have you downstairs. This is like old times." Jean had her knitting. She curled up on the couch. "Donna was skating and you should have seen her knees! It took me all this time to scrub them clean," she said.

"Remember when we used to skate?" Sue asked.

"I should say"; but Jean's tone of voice wasn't warm with remembering, it was almost patronizing, Sue thought. She saw Dan's eyes on Jean and looked away back to the fire.

"Happy, Sue?" Dan said. "You mustn't stay down too long at first."

Sue nodded. Was Dan happy? Were they ill at ease

with her here? Sitting here, knowing so much that they didn't guess gave her a feeling of power tonight. It was like a sharp weapon, a little dagger, hidden under her gown. She could hurt them with it; she could separate them forever . . . but that wouldn't give her Dan.

The doorbell rang and they all three sat as though stunned, waiting for something to happen. Then Dan went to the door and came back with a telegram in his hand. He stood in the doorway reading it.

But there was nothing that could come in a wire that would change anything for her, Sue thought. Jean looked up eagerly in a woman-habit of curiosity.

"It's nothing," Dan said. "The Maryland people wiring me that the deadline for their June number is May twelfth."

"That's day after tomorrow," Jean said.

Dan shrugged. "I'll wire them I can't do it: I wrote as much to them last week."

Sue was startled. "Why, Dan, isn't that the article you were working on the night I . . . I read proof?"

"Yes, but I've scarcely touched it since."

"Can't you do it tonight?"

Dan turned in surprise. "Well, if I worked all night I suppose . . . I don't care about it anyway."

He was on his way to the phone when Sue said, "You've worked all night before now." She heard Dan sending the wire. She was troubled. It hurt her to have Dan slip up on something.

Jean got up restlessly and pulled the curtains across the front windows. Jean's every movement was proprietary. It had become her house, Sue thought, and wondered that it did not hurt her more. Something had happened to Dan. He didn't seem to care about the paper . . . that wasn't like him. He used to have so much fire.

"Dan comes home tired out these days," Jean said, as though she were explaining him to her. "It hurts me to see him. After that Fairchild thing I wouldn't think he would need to do another thing."

Sue closed her lips on the words she could have said. She felt too tired to try to talk any more. She must go now before she was hating them again, before this room that she had made grew strange. Let them be alone. If they loved each other, if Dan had changed, there was nothing she could do about it.

"I think . . ." she began when Dan came back.

Dan came to lift her up before she had finished the sentence. The strength of his arms under her was sure, comforting. How quickly she changed.

On the stairs she leaned her head stiffly against his shoulder. Close to his ear she whispered, "I always like the ride home from a party best, Dan." "The ride"; she had to say it again.

"Oh, you do, darling, so do I," he murmured back.

She told Agnes to close her door when she turned out the light. She would not stoop to listen tonight for footsteps on the stairs, she told herself. But the sound of the car going down the drive came clearly to her through the open window.

"Jean, she seemed almost like herself tonight: as though she must feel every bit of her affliction."

"Oh, Dan, I don't think so. She seemed more like a child; the way she talked about skating and the way she watched the fire without seeming to listen at all."

"That's so," Dan said. But he thought of Sue whispering to him on the stairs, sense and feeling coming somehow out of that conglomerate stuttering of slurred syllables. "She seemed interested in my not getting off that paper," he muttered.

They drove for an hour, saying very little. Jean wondered if Sue would come downstairs every night now. If they would go on like this another year.

PART THREE

". . . this is that irradiation that dispels the mists of Hell, the clouds of horrour, fear, sorrow, despair; and preserves the region of the mind in serenity."

SIR THOMAS BROWNE
Religio Medici

THE sun was too bright on the open grass, so the breakfast table was set in the shade of the sycamore tree. The lilacs were in bloom, both the white bush near the hedge and the old sprawling purple bush by the porch. The crocuses made sudden spots of color along the flagstone walk. The forsythia was almost past; dozens of tiny blossoms littered the grass under the bush. Back against the fence a cherry tree was a pattern of white petals.

Dan and Jean were alone.

"It's heavenly, isn't it?" Jean dropped her head against the back of the chair. The sycamore tree laid its shadows on her face and across her shoulder. Dan's eyes were on her. She felt them even now with her eyes closed; but he didn't answer. She raised her head and looked at him. The tired, lean look of his face hurt her.

"Dan, you look so tired; didn't you sleep?"

He discounted her question, even her tenderness, with a slight movement of his mouth, a characteristic twitch of his nostrils. Dan could be surly. Jean wondered if Sue had ever seen him in a mood like this. But she didn't mind his surliness. For weeks now, ever since that walk on Good Friday, Dan had spoken scarcely an unnecessary word to her. He had finished breakfast when Donna did and hurried off half the time. He had sat upstairs with Sue, reading aloud to her; when they drove in the car he was so silent. But she understood. It didn't matter.

"Jean, let's get some people into this garden." His

outburst came so suddenly that it startled her. "I've sat here this spring till every bush has a thought on it, like a kind of blight."

She looked at him, wondering if he meant quite that, but Dan was busy with his pipe.

"All right," she answered. "This is Saturday; everyone's off this afternoon. We'll have a picnic lunch out here. Do you want contemporaries or the young fry?" Her tone was ironical at first, but she made it light again.

"The young ones, thank you, no contemporaries."

"We'll have it about one-thirty." She waited for Dan to call it off, but he didn't. He went up to see Sue.

It was two o'clock before every everyone was there: the Keiths and Kaplans, Tom Barton and the Whitneys, MacLean and the new Englishman from St. Bartholomew's whom Mac had brought with him. All the porch chairs were dragged down on the grass; Peter and Tom were stretched out on the ground.

Sue was there. Dan had carried her down in his arms and settled her under the sycamore before any of the others had arrived.

The food was set out on the big round garden table. Branches from the cherry tree filled the pottery dish in the center. Jean mixed the salad in an enormous bowl at one side of the table.

"Mrs. Norton's a delightful hostess," the doctor from Bart's said aside to MacLean.

MacLean smiled in a proprietary manner. "That's Jean Keller, Mrs. Norton's sister; she's priceless."

The others were scattered about in chairs and on the grass. Dan sat at Sue's feet with his back against her chair. Sue had a tall glass of iced tea with a straw that she sucked now and again, but mostly she held the straw with unsteady fingers and stirred the ice in the glass. She had had her lunch earlier, upstairs.

Sue was a little tremulous at first with so many people, but no one could notice that, she told herself. She sat very still so her arms wouldn't jerk so badly. Once without thinking she laid her hand against Dan's shoulder. Her arm moved stiffly but there was scarcely any tremor. Dan turned and smiled.

When Elsa Whitney sat down on the grass near her, Sue asked suddenly, "How was your trip to South Haven?" She had trouble with the words. She felt everyone listening. She saw the English doctor's eyes on her. But Elsa answered quickly:

"Pretty good, I guess. We decided to go there, but it's awful making up your mind!"

"What was it like, Peter?" Stan Keith asked. Everyone was interested. The mention of South Haven brought a feeling of impermanence to the moment.

"Well, Dr. Nelson seems to be the right sort and he has a good practice. . . ."

"Can't you see Elsa making the right contacts for Peter; making calls, going to bridge parties!" Sylvia Kaplan laughed.

Elsa made a wry face. "But it's a grand feeling to know where we're going to be next year."

Sue spoke again. Her voice did not sound so shrill out here. "I thought of you all day."

Dan was talking with Bernard Kaplan. Sue listened to them, thinking it was good to hear the medical shop talk that she had used to hear so much. She looked around the garden feeling herself aloof, separate from all of them, yet neither bitter nor lonely. If she could only keep this moment of serenity!

"This is the life!" Peter Whitney set his plate aside and rolled over on his back. He looked up into the sky between the twisted branches of the sycamore. He squinted because of the sun.

Stan Keith crept slyly up behind him and drew a blade of grass across his face. Peter brushed it off unconcernedly. He was listening to the young Englishman telling about a scavenging party they had had in London. Peter was content to lie on the grass with eyes closed and feel the sun beat down on him.

Stan crept forward again and drew the grass across Peter's face. This time Peter gave no sign of having felt it. But when Stan crept up again, Peter grabbed for his neck and pulled him head over heels on the ground. Stan yelled. Peter got away and dodged behind the trunk of the cherry tree.

"Get your man, Stan!" Dan called.

Peter circled around the lilac bush and slid behind

Sue's chair. "Save me, Mrs. Norton," he pleaded. gasping.

Stan stretched out on the grass. "Coward! I tell you my wind isn't what it used to be."

"I'm afraid you're slipping up on those periodic physical examinations, Stan!" Dan joked.

"You two babies, I could out-run either of you," Prue Keith announced, turning her knitting. Everyone laughed; Prue was such a picture of the poised young matron. She jabbed her needles vindictively into the ball of yarn. "Don't you wish we were the age for hide-and-seek and Prisoners' Base again?"

"And could run until you had a pain in your side and get so hot your hair curled around your face," Sue added very slowly, so wrapt in remembered feeling she was unaware of the self-conscious silence her voice had caused.

"Let's play hide-and-seek!" Peter suggested. "There's no age limit that I know of, and I'd like to see Prue out-run me."

The sycamore tree was goal. Prue was counting: "One, two, three, four, five, six, seven . . ."

All the others except Dan and Sue had disappeared. Thudding feet raced across the grass. A limb of the cherry tree shook dangerously and then was still. A tall figure appeared over the garage roof and then dropped out of sight. Dan chuckled.

"I only wish somebody like Hutchins would drop

in to call now, or our neighbor." He felt smoothed out and relaxed. He put his hand on Sue's knee.

"*The Strenuous Life*," Sue answered. It was an old joke between them. She had once found an under-lined copy of Roosevelt's book among Dan's things.

It had been a long time since Sue had referred to their old care-free days, Dan thought. Perhaps she was better. Perhaps this one summer they could have some semblance of normal living. Their sitting here, talking like this was so natural he could almost forget the nightmare of the last year. Through the smoke from his pipe he saw the garden lying in the sun. It was a different place from this morning.

"Ready or not, all around the by are it!" Prue finished triumphantly. She smiled at Dan and Sue and then disappeared around the house. The garden was still.

"Why don't you play, Dan . . . don't sit with me," Sue said laboriously.

Dan shook his head. "I'd rather sit on Olympus and watch the little mortals run."

The young English doctor loomed up behind the lilac bush and sauntered over to the sycamore. Prue had seen him and came racing around the corner of the house.

"Sneak-thief!" she called to him, as though he were a boy from another block. "Bern, I see you; you're behind the hedge. One, two, three on Bernard!"

Stealthily she crossed the grass and waited. Stan

came around the garage. From where they sat the spectators could see Prue and Stan approaching each other along opposite sides of the garage.

"Stan!" They raced to the tree. Prue's hair had worked loose from its knot. Her face was scarlet. She might have been Atalanta pursued by Hippomenes, Dan thought. He liked the figure.

"Atalanta!" he said to the young Englishman.

"She's not Atalanta, she's one of the Furies," the Englishman called out so Prue could hear. Prue made a face at him.

"Dr. Norton, didn't I touch goal before Stan?" she appealed to Dan.

Dan laughed and shook his head. "I'm not making any such decision as that. How about it, Sue?"

"No," Sue said, "Stan." But under her wavering monosyllables she was pleased to be drawn in to the fun.

Then Tom was "It." When a screen door banged sharply, he stopped counting to call out, "No fair in the house!"

Agnes had gone in for a sweater for Sue. Then slipping from nurse to child again, she went around the porch to hide back of the lilac bush.

The players were growing bolder. Dan grinned. "Don't you feel as though we were the king and queen having players perform a masque for us in our garden, Sue?"

Sue smiled. She hadn't seen Dan in such a mood for

so long. She watched Tom Barton chasing Elsa in to goal. She saw Elsa's slim young body that was so different from her own that was stiffened and shaky and helpless. "It's fun," she said.

Jean ran past. She looked as young as any of these girls. She had tied a bandanna under her chin like a peasant girl. The bottom buttons of her skirt had torn off and the skirt blew back showing her knees. She clutched at the skirt, helpless with laughter. Jean always could suggest a whole character by some little gesture. She slipped to her knees, now, in mock collapse, sucked her mouth in so it looked toothless, and groaned. Then she pushed her bandanna back on her neck and laughed.

"I'm ageing, there's no doubt about it." She dropped down on the ground, seeming more lithe because of her pantomime.

Everyone laughed at her except Sue. Sue glanced at Dan, but Dan had refilled his pipe. Now he sat calmly lighting it. He was not even looking at Jean. Sue's relief was tinged with shame. It was so hard to keep suspicion and hate out of her mind.

But Dan had been aware of Jean. He glanced over at her now, lying on the grass at the edge of the shade. He turned his eyes away from her. Half an hour ago he had been content, relaxed, feeling that his life was good here by Sue. Then Jean had run across the grass and his content was as completely passed as the brown, blistered blossoms of the forsythia bush.

"You're all hot. I'll go get some beer." Dan escaped into the house.

"Oh, that was fun!" Elsa said, sinking down in a canvas chair.

"This is probably the last time I'll ever play hide-and-seek," Peter observed. "I have a hunch that South Haven will expect sobriety from its leading practitioner."

Stanton and Tom had moved nearer. They were all gathered around Sue's chair.

"Do you know this is the second week of May?" Stan asked lazily.

"Don't bring Time into this day at all," Peter objected. "When we're hustling around in practice we'll appreciate this life here."

"I think I'll go to Europe and put off the evil day before I start practice," Stan said.

"You must come to Bart's then," the young Englishman put in.

"I shall," Stan said, then he added, "but I suppose I'm putting off the real thing all the time, trying to learn more. Maybe we've reached our capacity by now, anyway. What do you think, Dan?"

Dan poured a glass of beer with great care before he answered. "Stan, I don't think the choice you make at this stage of the game is half so important as you think it is. That was what I told Peter just the other day. You've all had a good foundation. Take anything decent that opens; the place and the circumstances will shape you to them if you're weak; you'll make them serve you if you're strong. That sounds like a mess of platitudes, but I believe it."

The young Englishman from Bart's uncrossed his long legs and leaned forward. "That's a dangerously individualistic doctrine for this day, Dr. Norton. That's the sort of exhortation the young men were turned out with a generation ago. Now . . ." he shrugged. "The world itself is worried and uncertain. I don't feel confident that I can shape circumstances to my liking. I feel I'm apt to be lost in the shuffle if I'm not killed in some war about 1940."

This was the sort of thing Dan loved. He shoved a little nearer and clasped his arms around his knees.

"That lost soul talk is from the defeatist school. Why should our profession get lost in the political and moral uncertainties of the time? Our guild has come down through all the political and social changes from the time of the Greeks." Dan's eyes flashed.

"There's no place in our curricula for the doctrines of defeatism. In a world of broken faiths, we have no creed and no duty except to use what knowledge and skill we possess to heal the sick and relieve the suffering."

Dan stopped abruptly. A curious instant of silence hung over the garden, a silence that was deeper than the mid-afternoon calm. The young Englishman's lips were pursed speculatively. The girls were listening, surprised at Dan's outburst. The men's faces were intent, thoughtful. Jean had scarcely heard Dan's words, but Dan seemed happier to her this afternoon.

Only Sue's face showed no reaction.

But her eyes watched Dan. He looked for the moment the way she had been trying to make him seem to her; not tired nor preoccupied, but eager. She could remember so many times when he had looked like that and talked like that, carrying everyone with him in his enthusiasm.

In the old days, she would have teased him about orating, when they were alone, very gently so he would know she liked it; but all that belonged to the old days. There was no time now to be playful with Dan. Everything they said was changed by her illness.

And she couldn't tease him about healing the sick; she was sick and Dan couldn't heal her. What a horrible joke it was on them both . . .

"Well," the young Englishman said with a smile, "if anything will save us it's that sort of faith."

Suddenly Sue laughed a foolish little laugh that ran into a strident mockery of a laugh. Her face reddened as though she were choking. She was having one of her dreaded laughing spells. She heard herself. She was spoiling everything. She had been so happy a few minutes ago. Now everything was ruined. She was crying at the same time. But she couldn't stop. She saw Dan's face, all their faces, trying not to look at her. She felt her own twisted in laughter.

Dan came to her quickly. The others made idle conversation among themselves. "Shall I carry you upstairs, Sue, where you can rest? I talked too much and wore you out."

"I'm all . . . all right," Sue said. "I was . . . just laughing." She went off again, hysterically.

"Sue, stop it, Sue!" Dan spoke very quietly, very firmly. Couldn't he see? She was trying so hard to stop. She felt humiliated in front of all of them. She hid her face against Dan's coat like a child. Dan slipped his arm under her and started to lift her.

"No, Dan, I don't want to go . . . leave me here," she protested. She didn't want to be sent off to bed. She mustn't go back to hide in her room. If she went now she would never try again. But she was so tired. She saw Jean glance at Dan pityingly. The old hate and rage welled up, making her laugh the harder. Then the laugh tapered off in mirthless hiccoughs. She closed her eyes in shame and weariness. When Agnes and Dan wanted to take her up stairs she shook her head. "Leave me alone," she managed wearily.

As though far away she heard the others leaving, saying they had enjoyed the picnic and the hide-and-seek, hoping they hadn't tired Mrs. Norton. The day that had been so idyllic had ended in a debacle.

She heard Donna: "Were you really playing hide-and-seek, Mac? Grown-ups don't play hide-and-seek!"

"Hush, Donna," Jean said.

When they had all gone, Dan carried Sue in.

"I'm such a load, Dan," she murmured as she felt

his muscles straining under the dead-weight of her body. And she thought with a hopeless pang that the burden of her illness was a greater strain on his spirit than the dead weight of her body on his arms.

2

MACLEAN and the young Englishman came back for dinner. Dan had invited them early in the afternoon when everything was going so well.

"Do stay; it's awful to have everybody leave at once," Jean had urged after an almost imperceptible pause. Dan seemed to crave people today.

But the dinner was not a success. They could conjure up none of the spontaneity of the afternoon. Dan was frankly quiet. The young Englishman was polite but sleepy. Jean and MacLean kept the conversation going.

After dinner Jean went out to sit on the porch with Dan and the Englishman. She seemed absorbed in their shop-talk but she was watching Donna. Donna had turned on the radio and coaxed MacLean to dance with her.

Donna's auburn head came only a little above his elbow, but he danced with her as though she were grown up. Donna's body was held very straight with a certain fawn-like grace. She was looking up at Mac.

When they came back out on the porch, Jean reached

out her arm in a rare gesture of tenderness. Donna came over and stood awkwardly by her chair. Jean pulled her down on the arm, but Donna's body was firm, almost resistant. Jean felt a sudden urge to say something that Donna would always remember, that would bring her closer before she grew too far away from her. But Donna reached down and scratched her leg.

"Gee, that makes the fifth mosquito bite." She seemed wholly child again.

"It's time for bed now, Donna. You take your bath and get all ready and I'll come up. Don't forget to go in and say good night to Aunt Sue." Jean could feel her voice growing parental; a vague unhappiness caught her thoughts.

She was talking as gaily as usual. She laughed at the Englishman's story. But she was glad when he and MacLean rose to go.

As soon as they had gone Dan said, "I'm going up to see Sue again; that was a bad outburst this afternoon, just when she seemed so much better."

"Well, I'm going to bed. Say good night for me," Jean answered, but the words seemed to leave something unfinished. After the ridiculous child's play of the afternoon their moods had degenerated into tired middle-age. She felt Dan's weariness more deeply than her own.

She met Agnes on the stairs.

"Mrs. Norton seems perfectly all right again, only tired," Agnes said. "Dr. Norton is going to sit with her until she gets to sleep. I'm going home for a little while."

Jean sat in front of her mirror brushing her hair. This was the place where she communed with herself. It was easier to know her own mind looking at her own image.

It would really be easier for Dan if she were not here. But she couldn't go away. She had to be here where she could see Dan. There were little things that she could do, that made his life more pleasant. When he came down from Sue's room tired out, sometimes she could change his mood. Dan was worried and harassed, but underneath, Dan must love her. That night after the bridge game she had been so sure. And he had said it would be intolerable without her.

Jean turned out the light and raised the windows higher. Outside in the dark she could see the lights of cars passing on University Avenue; lights streamed through the trees from some fraternity house. There was a feeling of stir and life in the May night that only deepened her own restlessness.

She got quickly into bed. But it was too early to sleep. She should have stayed downstairs longer. Perhaps Dan would go downstairs again. She lay in an attitude of sleep, but the first sound of a step in the hall brought her up in bed.

Sue had wanted even the bedside light turned off, so now Dan sat beside her in the dark.

He mustn't see her heavy face. She wouldn't talk. She found his hand and felt it tighten over hers. If they were still perhaps Dan would forget her fit of laughing. That night Dan had told her she could never bear children . . . couldn't Dan remember . . . they had sat together in the dark. They hadn't needed words.

"You must try your best to control that laughing, dear, it's so hard on you," he said gently.

"I know; it just starts, I can't help it, Dan."

He knew that and cursed his own foolish words. His pity for her rose so sharply in him he had to swallow it down. He was glad that the dark hid his face.

"I meant to tell you, Sue, I had a talk with Stephen today about you. He says you've made satisfactory progress. He says you're so much less nervous than you were." Dan closed his mind on all that Stephen had said: that the motor damage was greater, that each remission would be more brief, that her mind seemed less clear to him.

Sue only half listened. She was not interested. She was growing worse; the fit of laughter today was longer; it had left her more tired. There was nothing to do about it. But Dan . . . while she had strength she must hold him. He was far away again.

If he could feel that he really got through to her, Dan thought, but there was an unnaturalness about their talk together. Sometimes, she seemed almost like her old self. This afternoon she had said that about running; she had even teased him about *The Strenuous Life*, but those flashes were so rare. He wanted to ask her what she was really thinking, but he dreaded upsetting her again.

He tried talking about the afternoon in an attempt to break the heavy silence. He tried to make his tone jovial.

"I'll laugh for a good many years, Sue, over the picture of those youngsters playing hide-and-seek." Sue didn't answer. Up here the whole afternoon seemed far-away and completely childish.

He chose a safer subject: "Well, Peter got the place in South Haven! He seems quite pleased over it."

"Yes. I'm glad," she said.

"I must let you sleep, Sue." Sue was too tired to try to keep him.

Dan went down the hall to his own door. All the relaxation of the afternoon had gone for him with Sue's hysterical laughing attack. It was a hideous thing, Ophelia-like.

Now the noble words he had said to the boys gagged him. "The place and the circumstances will shape you to them if you're weak; you'll make them serve you if you're strong!" It was only looking at his young men, about to set out for themselves that had stirred him to any such pronouncement. Now, looking at his own life, the words seemed silly. Circumstances shaped you whether you were weak or strong.

His hand was on his own doorknob, but he turned and went instead to Jean's door. He hesitated outside and Jean spoke.

"Dan?"

He went in without answering. The room was half-lighted by the street-lamp on Willow Road. The light made the curtains and the bedclothes and Jean sitting up in bed, white. A ghostly patch of light was thrown across the rug. He crossed the patch of light and sat down on the edge of the bed.

"Jean, it's too much for me, sometimes."

"Forget about it for a little, Dan. You're tired out and you keep yourself going all the time. Having this crowd here today was idiotic." Her voice was understanding.

"No, I wanted them here," he said doggedly.

"Yes, of course, but you need to get away by yourself for a little. I'll go away, Dan, if I just complicate life for you."

"You mustn't do that; I couldn't go it alone," Dan said quickly. He turned to look at her. "Jean!"

"What, Dan?"

Dan could see her face, the line of her throat. Jean was still, waiting. She laid her hands gently on his face, smoothing out the weariness. He touched her lips, her shoulders, her breasts with hands made more sensitive by the feeling of Sue's rigid flesh. He did not say he loved her, but the hunger of his hands was enough. It was simple ecstasy to have him kiss her. She waited for him to come to her.

Then she felt the change in him even before he drew away from her.

"I can't do this, Jean." His voice sounded unnatural. He looked away from her across the shadowy room.

"Dan, we love each other . . ." but the sudden change she had felt in him stopped her. It seemed to her that he didn't hear her.

Dan rubbed his own hands across his face as though he meant to erase the feeling of her hands and their kisses. He went over to the door without a word, walking softly like a man in a trance.

It was more than an hour later that she heard the phone ring, the sound cut off so quickly she knew that Dan had been awake, too.

She heard Dan's voice, the click of the receiver, then Dan moving around his room. Finally, he came out and went downstairs. She followed him through the house by sounds: the sound of the swing door into the pantry, of the tap splashing in the kitchen sink. He was stopping now for a drink of water. She heard the back door and the door of the car.

She got out of bed and knelt at the open window in time to see him drive off towards University Avenue. Why hadn't she called him back? Why hadn't she gone to him? She knew she had been waiting for him to come back all this time until the ringing of the phone.

Dan let the car out. Keith had sounded worried, as though Peter were really sick. The urgency was good to feel.

He had not undressed. When the phone rang he had been sitting in the chair in his room, wondering why he had come away like that, like a boy afraid of himself. He wondered what Jean was thinking. Out here in the car, doing something, it was easier to think.

He tried to look at himself and Jean clearly, but there were so many tender places his mind shied away from. It wasn't that he had ceased to love Sue, he told himself over and over again. It was that her condition turned his love into pity; the fact that he could do nothing about it, but try to keep her believing that she was getting better, nagged at his spirit, depressed him, devitalized everything he tried to do. When she burst out in that senseless laughter she seemed like a total stranger. And when she lay staring at him, not speaking, she hardly seemed alive.

Jean was so alive to every mood and feeling. Jean loved him.

Dan lit a cigarette as he drove. To say that there was no difference between infidelity of the mind and body was stupid. Loyalty to Sue, some inherent moral sense had held him back tonight.

There was no need for self-deceit. There would be

another time and he might not be so strong. His mind rejected the word "strong"; it wasn't a question of strength. He was not naturally impulsive but controlled, disciplined. But, after all, he was no better than the next man, driven by loneliness and hopelessness. That was what sent a man to find comfort in someone else. It was nothing so simple as desire.

He threw his cigarette out of the car window. His thoughts went back to Jean. He saw her again as she had been this afternoon, dropping down on the grass, laughing. Could his loving Jean hurt Suc so much, after all?

He was glad to come to the Whitneys' house and be rid of his own thoughts.

3

ELSA opened the door before he could ring. "Dr. Norton, Peter's so sick!"

"When did it start?" Dan asked. "Peter seemed fine this afternoon."

"He didn't want anything but a glass of milk for supper and before I was through putting the baby to bed, he came upstairs. He said he had some cramps and that he'd be all right if he went to bed early. And then about ten, I came upstairs to bed and I heard him breathing hard, as though he were trying not to groan. He wasn't asleep; I could see that he was having a lot of pain, so I called Stan. I've never seen Peter sick before," she added by way of apology.

Stan came down the stairs. "Dan, I'm sorry to get you out, but I knew Peter would want you. He's more comfortable now, maybe it was just a false alarm."

Dan smiled quickly at Elsa. "Don't worry, we'll go up and have a look at him."

"Too much hide-and-seek, today, eh, Peter!" Dan began in a hearty tone, but he dropped it off as he stepped across the threshold of the bedroom. Peter looked sick. This afternoon, he had seen Peter stretched out on the grass in the sun; now he lay in bed, his color poor, his lips slightly opened, as though to ease his breathing.

"I don't know what struck me, Dan," Peter said, "but it seems to be a honey."

Dan went down to talk to Elsa. He found her sitting on the bottom step of the stairs in the dim hall.

"Elsa, I think Peter should go over to the hospital. I'm not quite sure what's wrong and it will do him good to lay up for a few hours while he's under observation. Don't worry, we'll take good care of him."

Elsa followed the curve of the newel post with her finger before she spoke. "I'll help him into his clothes," she said and ran upstairs.

Dan was up early the next morning. Jean's door was still closed. He looked in Sue's room. She was awake. He wondered if she woke early every morning and lay there like that, looking out the window. He went in and kissed her.

"Why, Dan, you're up early."

"Yes, Peter Whitney's sick. I saw him last night and sent him into the hospital. I want to get over early and see how he is this morning."

"How sudden," she remarked tonelessly.

"Yes, I rather think it's a kidney stone."

"Will he have to be operated?"

"I don't think so; not until the attack is over."

"Dan, don't let anything happen to him. He and Elsa are so . . . young," she finished flatly.

"I know, well . . . how are you feeling?"

Sue's mouth twisted in some slight semblance of a smile. "Better."

"Tell Jean I'll have breakfast over at the hospital."

Some anxiety, some shadow of depression he had taken from Sue stayed with him, mixing with his own thinking even at this minute. His own personal life had always been separate from his work; now it seemed always to be in the way of his work. Nothing was clear-cut any more. He wished now that he had left a note for Jean. He should have waited to see her at breakfast.

When he had seen Peter, Dan went to the smoking room to wait for Henry Brighton. He felt sure in his own mind, but it was a good idea to have a surgeon see Peter; that was what he always told his boys, and he had asked Henry to see Peter as soon as he came in.

Dan went over to the phone and dialed his own number. Jean answered. Her voice coming over the phone so clearly made him abashed.

"Oh, Jean, this is Dan."

"Yes, Dan." Jean's voice was low, responsive.

"Sue told you I wanted to get over to see Peter early?"

"Yes, how is he, Dan?"

"About the same. I'm waiting to see what Henry Brighton thinks about him. Jean, I didn't get back from the hospital last night until after midnight. Were you asleep?"

"No, Dan."

"Could you meet me at noon; we'll drive out in the country where we can talk."

As Henry Brighton came into the room, Dan said hastily, "About twelve-thirty, in front of the hospital." He hung up the receiver, conscious of a foolish trembling.

Stan Keith stopped in the doorway. When he saw Brighton he started to go.

"Come in, Stan. Dr. Brighton has just seen Peter," Dan called out. "Keith saw Whitney first last night," he explained to Brighton. "Well, what do you think, Henry?"

"If he had a zipper in his belly we'd have a look right now, but I think you're right, Dan; there isn't much justification for going in at present," Brighton said.

Dan nodded. "I think we better sit tight a while. His white count hasn't gone up since last night when we brought him in. There's a little tenderness on the right side, but no muscle spasm and the tenderness is pretty high for an appendix."

"Couldn't it be a high appendix?" Stan asked apologetically.

"I don't think so; that urine specimen certainly points to kidney and when that colicky pain is the worst it runs through the back and down. I'd hate to open up his belly and not find anything," Dan said.

"And then have to go to work on the kidney," Brighton added. "All right. We'll see what the white count is this evening."

Dan went on down to meet the class he was taking on the ward at ten. Henry was as good a surgeon as there was anywhere, he thought. He was glad Henry had confirmed his judgment. But minds were susceptible. He had an uncomfortable feeling now that perhaps he put the idea of kidney into Brighton's head. Not that Henry wouldn't discard the idea if his judgment were against it, but still he might have been predisposed by the note on the chart. As Dan went on the ward he thought wryly that if Peter were just a ward case, one of the younger surgeons would have gotten him and opened him up in a hurry without thinking much of a kidney possibility . . . and had the devil to pay.

Jean had walked over and was sitting in Dan's car when he came out of the hospital a little after twelve. Dan had just been up to see Peter and had ordered another white count at four. He had explained matters to Peter. Peter's trust in him was implicit. He was thinking of that now as he drove off.

"Dan, you look so worried; forget it now while we have lunch."

"I am worried. We're going to have another white count and if it's up at all, Brighton will operate."

"Well, any operating is up to Henry Brighton; let Henry carry some of the load."

Dan stopped the car on the bluff that overlooked the river. Jean didn't understand; he would never think of shifting the load to Henry or anyone else when one of his boys was in trouble.

Jean spread out the lunch things and poured the coffee. She was quiet, willing to follow Dan's mood.

"Jean, I stood outside your door for several minutes this morning. I don't really know why I didn't wait for breakfast. I wanted to tell you as soon as I got over to the hospital, I'm sorry about last night." He broke off as abruptly as he had begun and looked away from her.

Jean waited. At high noon in the bright sunlight the

stretch of green bluff and blue river managed to seem somber. Dan was silent. At last she burst out:

"Dan, why should you be sorry? Isn't it only natural that you should come to me when you're as disheartened as you were last night? It would be inhuman if we lived there together and meant nothing to each other!" Her voice that she had meant to keep calm was sharp. "Oh, Dan," she clenched her hands in her helplessness and then spread them out hopelessly. The strength of her feeling swept away her qualms. They must have each other; then they could stand the weary days of Sue's moods with patience. The way they were living was only an enduring that would squeeze them dry even of their love.

"Dan . . ." she said, not knowing what she would say, only that she must make him see.

"I know, Jean; don't let's talk, don't let's try to think," Dan interrupted. He gulped his coffee down and bit into a sandwich. He finished it and folded the wax paper in which it had been wrapped into a minute square.

"Another one, Dan?"

"No, thanks."

Jean put the lunch things away mechanically. Then she moved a little way from him and sat down against a tree. Her hands lay still in her lap. Dan was worried about Peter. He hadn't meant to shut her off like that, she told herself.

Dan was grateful for her silence. He took out his

pipe, sucked air through it to be sure it was drawing and then forgot to fill it. Sometimes he filled his eyes with Jean, sometimes he stared across at the valley until the whole view of rolling hills and blue sky and pale new green seemed to waver and shimmer out of focus like an amateur moving picture.

This morning he had felt he had to talk things out with Jean, but these things could not be settled by talk. He looked at his watch. "I've got to get back and have a look at Peter."

They stood up almost simultaneously. Jean picked up the basket. They had scarcely eaten anything.

Dan opened the door of the car for her and put the basket in back. She started to get in and some strangeness in their silence made her turn to look at Dan. Her face was close to his. He bent and kissed her. Then he put her into the car and went around to his own side. The leather seat was hot from the sun. Jean laid her palm against the burning surface happily, liking the sharpness of the stinging. If only they could drive away from the hospital, from Woodstock.

When Dan left Jean, he went at once to Peter's room without stopping on the out-patient floor.

4

THE laboratory reported a third white count while Dan was in Sue's room after dinner. Sue could hear his end of the conversation. It ended with Dan's calling Brighton and notifying the operating room.

"Brighton's going to operate, Sue," he said needlessly.

"But Peter will get along well, Dan . . . 'syoung 'n'strong," Sue said and the slurred words did not seem toneless in Dan's ears. But her confidence weighed on him.

"I'm going over to see what they find," he said as he left.

This was one of those warm May nights that seemed endless. Sue could see University Avenue as it always was in the spring: the girls and their men sauntering along to a movie or some place to eat. The porches of the fraternity houses would be full. In the library all the windows would be open. Some of the students would sit over their books with their fingers in their ears to block out the summer sounds of skating and cars and distracting laughter drifting past the windows. This summer she would ask Dan to take her out in the car again. She wasn't so sensitive now about people seeing her. It seemed childish that she had cared so much.

In the winter she had felt helpless. The fact that she

could never get well, the feeling of loneliness, the feeling of Dan's . . . there was no glossing over the ugly word . . . unfaithfulness had worked in her like poisons numbing her to any but her own interests, making her giddy with hate. But tonight she was drawn out of herself. She took delight in the May night. She was not sad or bitter or angry.

For the first time in months she felt close to Dan. Dan was worried, and his worry had taken her out of her own self-absorption as it always had. She could have laughed for sheer relief.

When Peter Whitney was well again she must talk to Dan, in spite of the way her words got mixed up and fell over each other. It was so easy forming the words only in her thoughts. They came smoothly this way: "You must keep faith with me, Dan, not just for me, but for yourself and your young men."

And they were true, weren't they? It wasn't just that she wanted them to be? They weren't just an excuse . . . she must be sure. There was such a thing as integrity . . . or wasn't there? Dan's own face yesterday, when he was talking about broken faiths, seemed answer enough. She must have it out with Dan. There had always been truth between them. "As long as I live, Dan . . ." she heard herself saying, and Dan would know all she had suffered.

But she mustn't say anything while Peter was on Dan's mind. He had been so worried tonight . . . he had always worried that way over his cases. It was as though their own lives stood still when one of his patients was in a critical condition.

Dan drove home after the operation. He was haunted by the extensiveness of the gangrene over that short a time. The delay had increased the danger, but it was a blessing it hadn't resulted in rupture.

He went back again over the whole course: the low white count, of course, and the pain high up, the urinary findings . . . he had been too sure it was a kidney. If anything happened to Peter, if he didn't make it . . . Dan's mind turned sickly away from that possibility; from the thought of Elsa.

He wondered whether Peter would have agreed with him on it. Peter always made up his own mind on things. He remembered the night in the hospital when Peter had worked over the man with the heart-failure. Well, he had used his own best judgment on Peter. He was right, usually. After all, that was the only measure of a doctor's skill; the proportion of rights he made.

Why was he worrying so? Brighton thought Peter would make it all right. The delay was partly Brighton's responsibility, but Dan's mind wouldn't admit that. If he hadn't said so much about the kidney, Brighton might have gone in at once. . . .

Dan drove around to the back of the house. There was still a light in Sue's room. He opened the screen door of the porch.

"Hello, Dan," Jean called from the swing.

"Hello, sitting here in the dark?"

"Yes, I couldn't settle down to anything. How is Peter?"

"Well, not too good. I think he'll make it, but he may have a stormy time for a while." Dan sat down in the chair wearily.

"Of course he'll make it, Dan."

Dan said nothing. Then he roused himself with an effort. "Sue must be still awake, I saw her light. I'll go up and say good night."

"How is Peter?" Sue asked slowly, as soon as he stepped into the room. Everyone was looking at him and asking him how Peter was.

"Not too good," he answered in the exact words he had used to Jean. "The delay didn't help any. It was an appendix; the thing was tucked way up behind the bowel where it had no business to be. That's why he had so few signs." He found himself going on in detail as though Sue were as interested as she used to be.

"Was it ruptured?" Sue asked, having trouble with the word, but Dan didn't notice.

"No, I honestly think he'll be all right. I suppose I just tried too hard to be sure."

He had gone on with his own thoughts when Sue said painfully, " 'Judgment is difficult.' "

Dan smiled in acknowledgment of the quotation. It was an old Hippocratic aphorism that he had taught her a long time ago. He came over to the bed. "Good night, Sue, you're as good a philosopher as Stephen." But he wondered that her mind had recalled it.

When he kissed her she would have put her arms around his neck, but she held them still because of their jerking.

Dan hesitated at the top of the stairs. It was close away from the windows. A suffocating stillness crowded the rooms on the second floor. Midway down the stairs, a certain fragrance of the spring night came up to him from the open door. But a heavy sadness filled his senses, as though borne in to him with that fragrance. Instinctively, Dan went through the house out to the coolness of the porch and Jean.

But they had little to say. Once Dan went in to phone the hospital. Peter was still under the anesthetic. He had vomited a good deal, but that was natural enough. If there were any change the nurse would call him.

Dan came back to the porch. He and Jean sat in the stillness with the dark, close house behind them. Dan was aware of Jean's hair, of the movement of her eyelashes, the slight rise and fall of her breast. He knew when she lifted one hand and laid it in her lap. It was a relief to think of himself and Jean for a minute. But his mind drifted back to the hospital and Peter.

"How is Elsa?" Jean asked.

"Worried," he answered shortly. "We all are. I've

tried to reassure her. I've seen plenty of worse cases get along well."

After a while Jean stood up, feeling that Dan wanted to be alone. "Good night, Dan, don't worry so. Let Henry Brighton carry some of that worry."

"Good night, Jean." Her last remark annoyed him unreasonably.

It was after three when the phone rang. It rang only twice before Dan was awake, but it penetrated the still house easily. Jean heard it in the room next to Dan. Agnes thought for a second that it was Mrs. Norton's bell. Sue was still lying awake.

Scarcely fifteen minutes later, Dan was out of the house. All the time that he could busy himself dressing, starting the car, making the sharp turn of the driveway, he could put off his fear. But driving smoothly along University Avenue in the soft dark it was before him.

The nurse had told him that Peter had come out from the anesthetic and had seemed all right for about two hours. Then he had complained of agonizing pain in his chest and now she could not rouse him.

The suddenness of the change suggested to him only one thing; but an embolus, he thought bitterly, a catastrophe like that, had no business happening to Peter!

He was aware again how he always imagined the worst on these anxious drives to the hospital in the early morning darkness.

Sue had lain still, listening to Dan going. She hated being in a separate room; not having Dan tell her as he dressed to go, about his call. He had been anxious she knew by the hurry in which he had left.

"Sue?" Jean opened the door softly. "Awake?"

Jean came in and sat in the chair by the bed.

"Sue, did you hear the phone ring? I'm so afraid Peter Whitney is worse."

"Yes . . . Dan went in such a hurry," Sue said.

"Dan feels it's his fault, Sue. He couldn't stand it if Peter . . . if anything happened to him."

Jean sounded as though she understood Dan, as though he were hers and she were explaining him to her, Sue thought angrily.

"Sue, he couldn't have made a mistake really, could he?" Jean asked it fearfully. She had been worrying about Dan. In spite of her anger Sue was touched.

"Of course he could," Sue said slowly, "but he did what he thought was best. That's all anyone . . ."

Her words took so long to speak that Jean couldn't wait. "But, Sue, he's been almost beside himself all day." Jean's voice was shocked. "It would break him up if . . ."

"No, he'd just have to stand it," Sue said. Jean didn't know about the time he lost the pneumonia case or the time . . . but words came too clumsily. It was too hard to explain. It wasn't a thing you could explain, even with all the glibness in the world. You had to be married to Dan, to have lived with him through those other times, to have watched him grow, to have gloried in his honestly putting his finger on his own mistakes.

"Dan's not . . . weak." She felt it triumphantly, but the words only sounded commonplace, spoken in her dragging voice. It was queer to hear herself say that.

Jean looked like a child huddled up in the arm chair, with her hands clasped around her knees. Sue had not thought of Jean as her younger sister for a long time.

"I know, Sue, but it would hurt him so!"

An unreasonable impatience made Sue say, "It will do more than that to Elsa if . . . if Peter should die." She felt a certain brutality. Jean was thinking only of Dan. Blind pity wouldn't help Dan. He wouldn't even want it.

"Could I phone and ask the nurse or someone how Peter is?" Jean asked a little uncertainly.

"That wouldn't do any good." Sue thought how used to waiting she was; how hard a thing it was for people to learn. She had never seen Jean so upset. Jean had always been self-contained about her own troubles, seeming even a little hard. Jean's love for Dan . . . she had hated Jean for it. She had not thought of it as something that softened her and made her sit crumpled up with fear for Dan. It was hard to hate her for it now.

They were quiet. Sue thought back to that night when she had listened to Jean's footsteps, her door closing, then Dan's. She had been rigid with hate and suspicion. Ever since then, she had watched Jean so narrowly for signs of her loving Dan. But now Jean sat across from her without any pretense, openly tormented and worried because she loved Dan.

"I wish Dan would phone us," Jean burst out.

"He wouldn't do that. He doesn't know we exist just now, either of us."

Then Sue said slowly, ponderously, only the meaning of the words making them stand out with terrible clarity in the dark: "Jean, you and Dan love each other."

She heard Jean catch her breath.

"Oh, Sue, I . . ." she broke off. "But Dan loves you, Sue."

"I'm so changed it's hard for him. He knows I can't ever get well." The slurred words spilled out in the shocked silence.

Sue felt Jean's arms around her. Jean was crying; trying to comfort her. She had always been the one to comfort Jean. Even now, the old instinct was strong.

"Everything will be all right, Jean," she said. The meaningless words couldn't ever be true for herself; perhaps they wouldn't ever be true for Peter and Elsa Whitney. Things didn't always turn out right, but she could bear it. Jean couldn't. "Don't cry, Jean."

Then some sternness impressed itself in her voice. "We mustn't ever bother Dan about any of this, Jean."

5

ELSA was having breakfast with Prue. Stan had gone over to the hospital and promised to phone from there about Peter. It was sunny in the dining-room. The sun on the yellow cereal bowls, on the plaid breakfast cloth was heart-warming. The morning paper was spread across the arm of Stan's chair. Little Peter sat up in his high chair and babbled gleeful noises just as usual. Fear and waiting and worry belonged to last night.

"It was absurd of me to need to stay with you last night," Elsa said. "I feel all right this morning."

"Don't be silly; you couldn't stay in that big old house with Peter sick."

"How soon after an operation do you start to feel better?" It occurred to Elsa that she knew very little about the ways of real sickness.

"Oh, I don't suppose for the first couple of days. Then we can start taking over good things to eat and detective stories," Prue said gaily.

Suddenly Elsa was impatient to get over to the hospital, to see Peter for herself. "Stan must be there by now; why doesn't he phone?"

Elsa lifted her cup to pass it, then set it down quickly. "Why, Stan is back already!"

"He had a bad night, Elsa, I thought you'd like to go right over," Stan said.

As they were driving over in the bright unreal world, Stan said cautiously, "Elsa, Peter's still unconscious. He won't know you yet."

"But shouldn't he be . . . isn't that a bad sign?"

"They're afraid he's had an embolus; you know, a clot."

Elsa asked no more questions. Fear settled down on her. The morning that had put courage into her had a false look. The hospital looming up as always at the end of the avenue was not Peter's hospital; it was an alien place, holding Peter in it, Peter who was so very sick.

They went up to Peter's door, but Stan took her to wait in the sunroom where she had sat yesterday. It was empty. The sun glared in brutally on her loneliness and fear. She sat on the edge of the settee. She pinched her lips together between her fingers to keep them steady.

Then Dan came out. Dan would tell her Peter was better. She went to meet him, scarcely knowing that she did so.

"Elsa, we've given him a transfusion; he's in the oxygen tent now. We're doing everything on earth to help him through." She watched his face that was so grave and worn. Her own face had gone white. She had trouble making words.

"I want to see him," she managed.

But Peter was separated from her by the cumbersome-looking paraphernalia and by the nurse hovering over him.

She went willingly when Dan led her out of the room back to sit in the sunroom. He explained Peter's condition; just what had happened, just what they had done. He told her truthfully that there was very little hope. He sat down beside her and let her cry against him.

The morning worked its way to noon.

A subdued sound of trays of crockery reached to the room at the end of the hall. Faint odors of food drifted through the air, cut across once by the terrible sweetness of ether and again by the harshly clean smell of an antiseptic.

Elsa was never alone.

Bernard Kaplan came and sat by her and gripped her hand so hard it was warm for a bit. Tom Barton came in, looking troubled and more disheveled than usual.

"Damn it, Elsa," he muttered, "if this isn't the damnedest thing!" He sat down in one of the squeaking rockers.

"Gosh, it's hot in here," he said after a minute, and got up to try each of the radiators in turn.

Elsa hardly noticed when he left, or when MacLean dropped in and brought her a cup of coffee.

Dan came again and stood beside her and she felt better when Dan was there.

Elsa looked down the length of the corridor that ran past Peter's door. The handles on all the doors were made like hooks. The tile of the floor was speckled gray and white with a black border against the walls.

A light over one of the doors flashed red. She had forgotten there were people back of all those doors. She had felt that Peter was the only one.

The light over Peter's door flashed. She ran to his door and pulled it open. Dan put his arm around her and drew her into the room.

When Elsa came out of the hospital, it was five o'clock. Cars were drawn up along the curb. There was Sylvia Kaplan waiting for Bernard.

Then it came to Elsa that she would never be parked out there in front waiting for Peter any more. Peter would never come out and look up and down for her and tease her about her parking and ask what there was for dinner. Peter was dead.

Dan and Stanton walked out to the car with her. They helped her in as though she were an invalid. When she was in the seat Dan took her hand in both of his. His eyes were wet. He turned away without speaking and Stan drove off. Stan was driving her to his house.

6

DAN went back into the hospital after putting Elsa in the car.

After the bright glare of the outside everything in the hospital was dark. The darkness obscured the faces of the people still waiting on the benches, the nurses coming along the corridor. Even the cherry-colored liquid in the big glass sphere hanging outside the pharmacy counter was dark. As his eyes grew accustomed to the dimness and the subdued light, this gloom became reality, the brightness of the outside world was the illusion.

On his way to his own office, the nurse at the desk stopped him. "Dr. Norton, I'm sorry, but there's a patient out here, a Russian woman who doesn't understand English very well. She says Dr. Whitney took care of her and told her to come back two days ago. She was back yesterday and today and I can't make her understand that . . ." The nurse left her sentence unfinished. "Would you see her? Dr. Whitney wrote on her record that she should have a cardiogram, but she says she won't until she talks to him."

There was no mistaking the woman; she sat stolidly, serenely waiting.

"Dr. Whitney wanted you to have a special test," Dan began.

"I wait, see Dr. Whitney." The woman looked away as though she would wait indefinitely.

Dan's voice was gentle. "Dr. Whitney won't be back," he told her. "He would want you to go right ahead with your tests."

"Dr. Whitney say he see me," she insisted. "I wait."

Dan's gentleness left him. "Dr. Whitney's dead," he told her sternly. "DEAD! do you understand?" As he said it aloud the full truth sank in upon him, too.

The woman's mouth fell open slackly. She crossed herself. She slid along the bench and getting up, went out of the hospital. Dan watched her lumpy figure disappear out the door.

When he turned the nurse was still hovering apologetically in the background. Her eyes were red.

"Dr. Norton, there's a patient who's been waiting to see you all day. I told her I didn't know when you'd be free, but she said she'd wait. Shall I tell her you've gone for the day?" she asked sympathetically.

"No," Dan said. "I'll see her."

He listened to the woman's heart and lungs, the long story she told of fatigue, colds, some fever. Very carefully he explained the course of treatment. At last, he was through.

Now the out-patient was empty; even the nurses had gone. The staff-room was empty, too. The rack was hung with fresh coats for tomorrow, each coat with the doctor's name printed on the pocket. There would be none with "Dr. Whitney" on it. The thought came dully into his mind.

He went into his own office and cleaned the desk of

debris. It had not been straightened for several days. He picked up an elastic band, a piece of waste-paper, tore the day off the calendar pad. Peter Whitney had died on the seventeenth of May.

Then there was nothing more to keep him. He changed into his suit-coat and went out to the car.

Dan drove home slowly. The world lay as he had known it so many springs before: gay, green, waiting. Now the students loitering along the walks in all their youth might have been figures on a Grecian urn, so meaningless they were to him, so remote. He felt a quietness in the twilight that spread from the high, light sky down upon the old streets. The very life of another spring made the burden of Whitney's death seem heavier.

He started to go over those first symptoms again but he stopped himself forcibly. It would only make him shakier the next time his judgment was on trial.

Jean came to him as he opened the screen door. She seemed cool and lovely, blessedly removed from sickness and death.

"We lost young Whitney," he told her before she could ask.

"Yes, Tom telephoned Agnes," Jean said. "You're tired, Dan; supper is ready out on the porch. Do you want to eat now?" Dan seemed different. She felt ill at ease with him for a moment.

He had no desire to eat, but the idea of being dramatic, of showing how deeply he felt Peter's death was repellent to him.

"All right," he said.

The porch was so shielded by vines that the candleflames on the little table barely flickered. Dan sat down. He drank his glass of water.

"We should have gotten at him sooner."

"You mustn't blame yourself, Dan; it wasn't your fault," Jean said quickly.

"Yes; it was my fault, my responsibility, anyway."

"Oh, Dan, that's absurd. You did what you thought was best."

Jean's tone dismissed his responsibility too easily. He made no answer. He ate without knowing what he was eating.

Jean began talking in a different tone. "Charlie cut the grass today. Donna had a wonderful time running barefoot on the lawn . . .

"Oh, Mrs. Clark stopped on her way downtown and said she and Dr. Clark were consumed to know what kind of a party we had over here Saturday afternoon. She said every time they looked over someone was racing madly around the house. Imagine how she looked, Dan, when I told her we were playing hide-and-seek! I said that you had been entertaining the younger group." Jean laughed. Dan smiled. Then they both thought that Peter Whitney had been playing hide-and-seek on Saturday, and they were silent again.

"I wish we could get away together for a whole day, Dan," Jean said, looking at the weariness in his face.

"That wouldn't help any," Dan said shortly. He knew Jean was trying to divert and comfort him. But she was trying to make the two of them important, and they weren't important tonight. There were times when their interest in each other, their desire had no place. He couldn't come from watching Peter die and sit here talking about themselves. Jean didn't understand.

She came over to him and laid her hands on his face as she had the other night. She kissed his forehead.

"Dearest," she said, "you mustn't worry any more. It's over now."

"Dan, Peter can't be dead!" Elsa had sobbed, clinging to him in Peter's room. Dan winced. He pushed back his chair.

"I'm going up to see Sue," he said. He didn't see the hurt in Jean's eyes.

Jean carried the supper things out to the kitchen and came back to the porch to wait for him.

7

HELLO, Sue." He made an effort to have his voice sound cheerful.

"Oh, Dan, I've been waiting for you." Her words slurred badly. They were without inflection. He bent and kissed her as he always did. Tonight her hand jerked out to touch his arm. "Sit down a while, Dan."

He pulled up a chair and sat by her bed. He forgot to talk at first in his utter weariness.

"Dan, I'm so sorry about Peter."

He laid his hand over hers on the bed. Then something in Sue's gaze that was so stripped of all quick expression, so dulled, made it easy to get his self-accusation into words.

"Sue, it was my fault," he said abruptly, finding his mouth dry as he spoke. "He should have been operated sooner. I held off, thinking it was a kidney. He might be living if I hadn't persuaded Brighton to wait."

"I know, Dan," Sue said simply.

She didn't protest. She seemed to accept the fact that he had made a mistake. She cared, he knew, as much as he did. He forgot that he had thought her mind was dulled.

He was silent so long that Sue thought he had forgotten her, that he was suffering over Peter's death, but she left him alone, content to be with him.

"That's what you used to say, Sue, remember?"

Sue's eyes smiled.

"I remember the time, Sue, when you sat on the front stairs in your nightgown while I told you about my pneumonia case; the one I thought I might have saved if I'd given the serum earlier. Funny, I was thinking of that just the other day."

Dan remembered, too. She had thought he was too taken up with the present.

"I guess I must have made you suffer with me on every one of my wrong judgments."

She wouldn't try to talk. Her voice got so in the way.

"But I've never lost a case that hurt so much, Sue."

Then her thought forced its way into words in spite of their slurring.

"Dan, it's such a pity that Peter should die . . . when I . . . go on living. Elsa . . . must feel it's . . unjust. Everybody must . . ."

"Don't talk that way, Sue," Dan said sharply.

She brushed his protest away with a jerking movement of her hands.

"I've known a long time now that I couldn't ever get well . . . I'm used to the idea." The words came very slowly, without expression. She forgot that she had meant to use that knowledge to hurt him. "I wish you could have traded me for Peter."

Dan was shocked out of his own thinking. He made an inarticulate sound.

Of course she must have guessed the hopelessness of her condition in spite of their careful pretenses. She had lived too long with him in a medical atmosphere to be deceived. She had kept the knowledge of her incurability to herself while he was preoccupied with self-pity, while he was turning to Jean.

He had no words; he was too choked by remorse and pity. He laid his head against her hand on the bed.

"Sue . . ." he hesitated.

"I know," she whispered. He mustn't tell her anything. There was no need. She didn't want him to be ashamed or sorry for needing Jean. She didn't want him to be sorry for her. She only wanted to feel that he was hers.

"Sue . . ." he tried again. But how could he tell her that seeing her change until she seemed a stranger, that trying to act as though she were getting better had taken the life out of his days until he had lost interest in his work. How could he tell her about Jean?

Sue lifted her hand toward the light switch. Her hand jerked so badly it shook the bed.

"Light out, Sue?"

She nodded. "I want you to forget for once how I look, Dan."

"Sue! Look at me, under the light!" He looked into her eyes that were as bright as they had always been, at her high white forehead under the dark hair. "Sue, I can see only your eyes. Your eyes haven't changed." He kissed her eyelids, feeling his own eyes sting.

"I haven't changed, Dan." Now when she cared so much, her words were almost unintelligible. But Dan understood.

"No, Sue." He was thinking that he was the one who had changed, or had he really?

"Dan, it's so hard for you. I've seen . . ." she left her sentence unfinished; words came too clumsily. They were quiet again. He turned off the light.

Sue was glad that she had never told him she knew

about Jean. And Jean must never tell him. It was unimportant. He was hers. Nothing could separate them, not even change or illness. All year she had envied Dan's young people, now that envy dropped away. Her life and Dan's had gone so far beyond theirs. And Jean; Jean was just one of Dan's young people.

Dan broke the long silence. "Remember our first year here, Sue, in the old Abernathy Apartments?"

He felt the pressure of her fingers on his. He was remembering the night he had tried to comfort her over her childlessness. They had sat together like this. It had been just such a spring night. She had been afraid he would feel cheated. He had never felt cheated; their lives had been too full; and even now, Sue . . . Why, Sue was even now his very peace of heart and mind.

"Sue!" His arm around her was too eager to be wholly gentle; his lips were too hard. And when he kissed her, it was not for pity.

Long after the room was dark Dan sat beside the bed. Whenever Sue stirred, he touched her gently. They were not aware of the restless sounds of the May night.

Dan must have gone on to bed, Jean thought. It was so late; he wouldn't come back down now. She latched the screen door and closed the house for the night.

"Let me not to the marriage of true minds
Admit impediments. Love is not love
Which alters when it alteration finds,
Or bends with the remover to remove:
O, no! it is an ever-fixed mark,
That looks on tempests and is never shaken;
It is the star to every wandering bark,
Whose worth's unknown, although his height be taken.
Love's not Time's fool, though rosy lips and cheeks
Within his bending sickle's compass come;
Love alters not with his brief hours and weeks,
But bears it out even to the edge of doom.
If this be error, and upon me prov'd,
I never writ, nor no man ever lov'd."

WILLIAM SHAKESPEARE, *Sonnet CXVI.*